SUNDOWNERS

IRON DRAGON

Fivehawk gave a solemn nod. "It knows we are here, like a spider senses vibrations in its web."

"Ah, don't get all spooky on me!" Tyler growled. "A train is a piece of machinery. It's not alive. It's just a big piece of pig-iron on wheels!" He slapped his hand on the wall to illustrate his point. "See? Not alive!"

At that moment, the Black Train's ear-splitting whistle screamed through the air like a banshee wail, and a spasm rippled down the length of the carriages. With a crunch of metal on metal, the train began to inch forward on the rails.

Yu Lim and Fivehawk favoured the white man with hard stares and he blinked back at them. "Uh," he managed. "Right?"

Have you read the other books in the series?

Ghost Town
Underworld

And coming soon:

Showdown

Point

SUNDOWNERS

IRON DRAGON

James Swallow

SCHOLASTIC

Scholastic Children's Books,
Commonwealth House,
1–19 New Oxford Street,
London WC1A 1NU, UK
a division of Scholastic Ltd
London ~ New York ~ Toronto ~ Sydney ~ Auckland
Mexico City ~ New Delhi ~ Hong Kong

First published in the UK by Scholastic Ltd, 2001

Copyright © James Swallow, 2001

ISBN 0 439 99213 3

Typeset by
Cambrian Typesetters, Frimley, Camberley, Surrey
Printed by
Cox & Wyman Ltd, Reading, Berks

10 9 8 7 6 5 4 3 2 1

1: A LAND WITHOUT GHOSTS

The sky was a vast cowl of grey, oily wool strung out over the mountaintops, the invisible sun casting a weak light in all directions across the hardened, chilled landscape. The work camp had been in this spot for a little over nine days now, the labourers slaving under the shadow of the mountain the white men called Frost Peak, the endless grind of stone and the clanking of metal against metal echoing around them. Yu Lim peered out from under her battered straw hat and shivered. Here in this place there was never enough warmth to go around, never enough food or water. This land, this America, was a cold, cold place, and not for the first time she longed for feel of her homeland beneath her feet instead of this iron-hard earth. Hundreds of her people were here, silently carrying out their duties, gradually assembling the lengths of steel track and wooden sleepers, building the railroad that wandered back and forth through the foothills. She moved quickly between the shacks and tents that formed the camp's nucleus, vanishing into shadows whenever one of

1

the lumbering hulks that guarded them hove into view. Yu Lim allowed herself a small smile. From the day she joined the ship at Shanghai, she had made herself invisible to these overseers, these outriders. The teachings of her elderly *sifu*, her teacher, were second nature to her now, and she could make her footsteps quieter than a cat's, should she desire. But she had wasted too much time; Yu Lim had allowed herself to become distracted by her concerns for her brothers and sisters, who slaved and slowly died as they forged the iron road – and for what? The railroad led nowhere, it did nothing. She shook off the thoughts, blinking them away like tears from her eyes. Her purpose here was clear, and it was time for her to fulfil it.

Tong Biao was a stocky, middle-aged man with wide eyes and an easy smile, even in a place like this, and he never failed to make Yu Lim grin whenever she stole out of the shadows. Startled, he coughed and blinked, and caught a squeal of alarm in his throat.

"Yu Lim, you are a demon child!" he hissed. "Why do you find such amusement in scaring me?"

"Ah Tong, I take a smile where I can."

"Indeed." He nodded, then looked away. "Come, then. Let's do this before I change my mind."

Tong led Yu Lim to a canvas-covered wagon stacked with long cloth sacks. The girl shuddered at the sight of them; each one contained a corpse, a worker who had fallen victim to an "accident" or other misadventure. From the back of the wagon emerged Sing Lung, a younger man closer to Yu Lim's age, but worn down by a life of hard toil.

"More victims of the sickness," Sing said carefully.

Yu Lim nodded. All through the camp, the workers whispered about a disease, unseen and deadly, that stalked them. Its prey would slowly sicken and die, as if the very *qi* – the essence of life – was siphoned from them.

"Where should I hide myself?" she asked, putting aside her concerns.

Tong Biao shifted from foot to foot and shook his head. "This is not right. You are a child. You should not be here."

"I have no choice," she said carefully, and sighed. "Ah Tong, we have had this argument a hundred times and still you wish to have it again."

"She knows what she must do," Sing Lung broke in, producing an empty sack.

"I do," Yu Lim said, and she leant close to Tong. "Trust in Heaven." She planted a kiss on his cheek and stepped into the sack. "Quickly, now. Red-hair will be here soon."

Sing Lung took a quick look around to make sure no one was watching them, then pulled the sack up around her. He paused before closing it over her head. "Do you have it?" he asked.

3

She nodded, showing the tip of a long object wrapped in cloth, hidden in the folds of her jacket. "It has never left my hands."

He nodded and closed the sack over her. His pleasant face now a scowl, Tong Biao took Yu Lim's legs while Sing Lung held her arms, and they gently placed her atop the pile of the dead.

"Good luck, little sister," Tong mumbled.

"The nimble foot gets in first." Yu Lim's voice was muffled, but it carried an edge to it. "Fear not for me, my friend. I have no path other than this one."

Tong opened his mouth to say something else, but Sing Lung grabbed his arm and pulled him away. "The Red-hair is here!"

They rode into the camp on five horses all black as pitch. At the fore, two outriders cast watchful stares out over the workers as they paused in their labours, and riding behind was a trio of women. Sitting high in the saddle, Red-hair's flame-coloured tresses cascaded down her back like a fiery waterfall, fanned out over the long ebony leather coat she wore. The sight of the woman always disturbed Tong Biao; a thick blindfold covered her eyes and yet she moved as if she could see more than any of them. The outriders dismounted, and then the other two females, before Red-hair stepped down. Tong studied the women. They were similar in stature, long and willowy in a way that the girls he'd chased during his youth in Canton never were. One

4

was as pale as milk, with a face framed by yellow curls, the other tawny-skinned with dark hair. Both of them had eyes that pierced anyone who met their gaze.

Red-hair was speaking to another outrider, a bearded man who seemed only shades away from an animal up on its hind legs. "Grizzly, you have done well. Master Drache is pleased with your work here."

The outrider scratched at his face. "I work these Chinee real good, ma'am."

"You do. We will soon be finished."

Tong Biao's heart jumped in his chest. Finished soon? Then perhaps he could still save Yu Lim from her dangerous outing...

Sing Lung's hand clamped around his arm. "Stop it, Ah Tong! I know what you are thinking! Don't let your feelings cloud your judgement!"

One of the outriders began to hitch his horse to the canvas wagon, and he gave the two men a sneering glance.

Tong rounded on the younger man and snarled, "She's just a girl! Someone filled her head with silly stories, made her come halfway around the world, and for what? Enough of our people have come here and died here, so why add another?" He spat. "When we came to this America, we called this place the Land Without Ghosts because no Chinese had been buried here, but that's not true any more!

We're filling it up with our dead!" He pointed at the wagon. "She'll join them!"

Sing Lung cast a nervous glance at the outrider, then back to Tong. "Quiet, you old fool! No man can argue against the orders of Heaven! You'll draw them here and they will kill her for certain!"

The anger suddenly fled from Tong Biao. "Oh, Ancestors. What am I doing?"

"Dawne, what are they saying?" Red-hair's voice demanded. Sing and Tong froze.

The pale woman studied them. "I'm not sure. Something about death."

"Indeed?" Red-hair said nothing, but the dark-skinned woman stepped closer to examine the wagon. Red-hair nodded. "Perhaps they are mourning a friend? Duske, we wouldn't want to send anyone to their grave before their time, would we?"

The dark female nodded, and drew a thin, rapier-like blade from a scabbard under her coat. Sing caught a glimpse of a strange, jewelled clasp in the woman's hair before she stepped on to the wagon, and drove the blade hilt-deep into one of the corpses. Then the next. And the next.

Tong Biao was not really aware of what he was doing until the stone was in his hand, scooped up from the muddy, cold earth at his feet. In a blur of movement, he shoved Sing Lung to the ground and let the rock fly. It described a perfect arc and crashed into Red-hair's temple, knocking her off her feet and to the ground. Duske and Dawne both twitched, reacting to the impact.

"Ah Tong, you madman!" Sing Lung gasped.

Grizzly was suddenly at Tong's throat, his meaty hands grabbing him; the big man moved like lightning, dragging him to where Red-hair was getting back up.

Dawne reached out to help her, but Red-hair waved her away, dabbing at the wound on her head with the cuff of her coat. "You dare strike Targa, your governess and beloved benefactor?" Red-hair hissed the last word like a curse.

Tong Biao's bravado faltered in his chest. "Tuh-Targa?"

Her lips parted in a thin smile. "You know my name, Chinaman. Good." She traced her stained fingers over his face, and to his horror, Tong realized that her blood was not red, but a dark green. "You'll die with it on your lips."

She embraced him, and Tong convulsed. From his place in the mud, and through a tiny rip in her sack, Sing Lung and Yu Lim saw their friend die as a single shot rang out. Tong stumbled backward, revealing a smoking derringer in Targa's fist.

As one, Duske and Dawne each took an arm and carried Tong's cooling corpse back to the wagon. Sing Lung blinked back tears, too afraid to speak or move, and watched them toss him on to the pile of the dead.

"What about the other bodies?" Grizzly ventured.

Targa's hidden gaze settled on Sing Lung. "Dead now or dead later is still dead. Go feed the mountain."

With the crack of a whip, the wagon lurched away; inside, Yu Lim cried silently as Tong Biao joined her for the journey up Frost Peak.

"Could it get any colder?" Tyler gasped, his words turning into puffs of white vapour. "I've never been this cold in all my life."

"Perhaps if you keep talking, you might warm up from the exercise. You are certainly moving your mouth enough." Riding alongside him, Fivehawk kept his usual tone of casual indifference.

Tyler scowled. "You Indians are way too cranky, you know that? I mean, you make everyone think you're calm and collected, at one with nature and all, but underneath it you're just plain ornery!"

Fivehawk sniffed. "I am not 'ornery', as you put it. I am just able to keep my mouth shut for more than two minutes."

"Bah," said Tyler, and shivered. They had been riding steadily northwards for days since they left the valley of the Hidden People, the dusty, arid desert slowly giving way to rocky scrubland and eventually the hills and mountain ranges that now surrounded them. Each day, it seemed like the chill in the air edged a little deeper into Gabriel Tyler's bones, and he chided himself for all those times in his life that he had ever complained about hot days and sunburn. Fivehawk seemed to rise above it all and never appeared to shiver – some secret Indian trick, no doubt, Tyler decided. Not for the first time, he found himself wondering why he had volunteered to join the wanderer on his quest; one might have said it was fate that brought them together, both of them searching for a lost family member. They had found a trail, all right, and it had led them to Stonetree, a town emptied of its citizens by one Robur Drache.

Tyler flinched again, and this time it wasn't because of the cold. Drache. The name hung heavy in his mind like a storm cloud, a dark, baleful presence. The cowboy flicked a glance at Fivehawk. The Indian swore blind that the ruthless rail baron was hardly a man at all, more a demonic figure in league with something even worse than he ... and after the strange things Tyler had seen in the last few months, even against his better judgement he was starting to believe that there was something to Fivehawk's words. He'd fought dogs that seemed spawned from the mouth of Hades itself; shot a man dead and seen him rise up for revenge; even ventured down a mine that could a have been a conduit to the underworld. He chewed his lip. These and all the other peculiar happenings were things a man might see and go crazy in spite of it, all of them thrown into his life since the day he met Jonathan Fivehawk. And yet, he would never have found his paternal Uncle Bill if not for him, would never have rescued the old man who raised him from a boy from a life of slavery. Now this was Fivehawk's quest, his search for his sister, and darn it if Tyler didn't hear that nagging voice in his head telling him that yeah, he owed this uppity, insufferable redskin a debt, and finding this girl would square it, once and for all.

As for Drache... Well, they would burn that bridge when they came to it.

Fivehawk gestured. "There's a town ahead."

Tyler dismissed his thoughts and followed the Indian's outstretched hand. The mountain pass they had travelled through was opening into a valley of grey earth, skeletal trees and white drifts of snow. The vista was dominated by a huge craggy mountain that climbed into the sky like a tower, and at its base, a cluster of shapes peeked out of a light mist. A town, all right, but a small one at that.

"Good enough," Tyler breathed. "Just thinking about a warm bed and a glass of whiskey makes me feel a whole heap better."

"We're not here to indulge you." Fivehawk's words held an edge of irritation.

Tyler sighed. "We can't look for her if we're both frozen to death, now can we? Listen, we'll take a room, get a good meal, ask around and then move on." He waved a hand to indicate the landscape.

"These mountain towns all know each other's business. If someone here has seen or heard of Drache, we'll know about it."

Fivehawk gave a non-committal grunt and they rode on.

The road into the town wound around a pair of foothills and through a ragged colony of white tents scattered across a muddy field. There were dozens of people there, cooking food or stoking campfires, but all of them fell silent as Tyler and Fivehawk rode by. It took a moment for Gabriel to realize that there wasn't a white face among them.

"The people," Fivehawk whispered, "they have skin like straw."

Tyler nodded. "Ain't you ever seen a Chinese before?"

"Chy-nees?"

"From China. These folks are brought over to work on the railroads, see, to earn some money and find a new life, this being the land of opportunity and all."

"But where is their homeland?"

Tyler pointed eastwards. "Clear around the world, Fivehawk. I hear tell that they live with a whole family in just one room..." He paused, studying the thin tents. "Can't say as this looks much better, though."

The Indian looked solemn. "No man should live like this, no matter where he comes from."

Ahead, a tall archway announced the town proper, displaying the name in wooden letters laced with frost.

"Winterville. I wonder why they named it that." Tyler grimaced. "C'mon, let's find a place to warm up before I freeze to my saddle."

There was only one hotel in town. Like all the buildings along Winterville's streets, it was a chunky, squared-off wooden construction, cut from huge logs and salted with patches of clinging snow and icicles. The hotel – the faded sign outside called it an "inn" – was one of the few buildings with two storeys, and it faced outward from the town centre. Tyler caught sight of a water tower in the distance and nodded to himself.

"There's a railroad station here, looks like. That explains the tents."

Fivehawk dismounted quickly. "I'll see to a stable. You find us a place to sleep."

Tyler took a moment to straighten his coat and stepped into the inn. It was warmer inside, and he blinked as the temperature change brought tears to his eyes. Here and there, a few grey-faced locals looked up at him with hollow eyes before turning back to their drinks or card games.

"Oh, this town is full of live ones," he told himself, and approached the bar. A skinny old man, barely a bag of bones in an apron, gave him a sideways glance.

"What'll it be, mister?"

"Whiskey." He dropped a quarter on the counter. The coin vanished into the bartender's hand to be replaced by a shot-glass full of amber liquid; Tyler dashed it back and coughed.

"You want another, that'll be another quarter."

"That's steep!"

"Railroad tax, is what it is. Pay up or ship out."

Tyler scowled. "Just that one will do, then. How much for a room, two beds? I'm almost afraid to ask."

"Buck and a half a day. Plus a dollar railroad tax."

Tyler shook his head and reluctantly handed over the money. "It better have silk sheets and hot water."

The old man grinned, showing too-few brown teeth. "Follow me. You'll need this too." He passed over a tin bucket.

"What's this for?"

"The leak."

Tyler snatched the bucket from the old man and walked after him, as Fivehawk entered. The Indian looked at the bucket and raised an eyebrow.

"Don't they have an outhouse here?"

The room was cramped and draughty, but the bartender showed it off as if it were a suite at the Peabody. "Stove over here to keep you warm, beds fumigated so there's no lice and a nice view of the Governess's house."

Fivehawk peered out of the window; a few streets away, an ornate building with a high fence and barred windows sat amid a copse of leafless trees. The house seemed strangely out of place in Winterville, as if it had been plucked from a New Orleans back street and dropped into this chilly little town. Then something caught his eye: a dark shape in the distance. The Indian grabbed at Tyler's saddlebag and pulled out his spyglass.

"No cooking food in the room. Clean sheets are a dollar," the bartender snapped, and closed the door behind him.

Tyler slid the bucket under the dripping leak from the roof and began to build a fire. "Railroad tax, my eye. That old coot gouged us but good!"

"Tyler. Come here."

The cowboy looked up; Fivehawk was at the window, the telescope set on something out at the edge of town. "What is it?"

"See for yourself."

Tyler squinted through the spyglass and his breath caught. At the railroad spur close to the water tower a massive machine sat on the tracks, a huge ebony bullet on wheels, emitting thin wisps of steam. "Drache's locomotive."

Fivehawk nodded. "The Black Train. Drache is here. We've found him."

Yu Lim could not see where the wagon had halted,

but something told her that her destination had not been reached. The air was thinner here, telling her that they had moved higher up the mountainside, and yet they were still far short of the top. She was drawn there, compelled to search out the evil she knew lurked in the grey clouds that wreathed it. Even from far below, she had been able to see the glittering lights from the peak. As she crept unseen around the camp, her grasp of the white man's language had allowed her to listen in on the outriders' conversations, and little by little, Yu Lim assembled the fragments of a plan. This being, this man-who-was-not-a-man called Drache, hid up there, building his steel rails and planning dark things. She touched the cloth-bound object under her coat and nodded to herself. She would bring the mountain down upon him or die trying.

There was a squeak of wood from the front of the wagon. The outrider was moving. She heard a snort from his horse, and suddenly the carriage shifted – it was moving backwards! Yu Lim pulled at the sack and it ripped open, allowing her to see. She gasped as the view through the open end of the wagon changed; the snow-covered path moved out of sight, to be replaced by the yawning gash of a crevasse.

Targa's words returned to her: "Feed the mountain." With sudden clarity, Yu Lim knew exactly what that meant. She had secreted herself aboard the wagon in hopes that the bodies were being taken to Drache's mountaintop eyrie, but the fate of the honourable dead was now very clear to her indeed.

The outrider, a stony-faced man who called himself Heller, paused as the wagon settled into the spot where he'd brought it so many times before. He grabbed at a protruding lever and yanked on it, hard. Beneath the frame of the wagon's bed, a cogwheel and latch spun open and the canvas-covered carriage tipped up at a steep angle. One by one, the cloth-shrouded corpses began to slide out, over the lip of the chasm and down into the icy grasp of the ravine.

Yu Lim held on to part of the frame as the wagon disgorged its contents. She almost held out a hand to stop Tong's body from falling away, but held back – his weight would have been enough to drag her out after him. For a moment, the panel held her, but then a splintering crack, loud as a gunshot, echoed around her. The wooden stay bowed and split, bending along its length. Outside, Heller gave the wagon a kick to dislodge what he thought was a stuck body.

Her hands were cold and numbed even through her woollen gloves, and when she lost her grip, she never even felt it go. The wagon spat her out into the frosty air and she fell, arms wide like a bird's spread wings, headfirst into the drifts of snow that lined the canyon's icy walls.

2: CONFRONTATION

At its fullest height, Frost Peak was bathed in an eternal twilight, the blunt prow of the mountain forever concealed inside a crown of grey mist. It was never a clear day up here, in this thin, chilled air where workers and outriders toiled alike among glittering gas lamps and great arches of black iron. If one could have dispersed the mist with a sudden gust of wind, the extent of the construction on the peak would have been clear for all to see. At last taking shape now, after months of work and toil, was the Terminus. It resembled the ornate glasshouses of the Great Exhibition, a dome of tinted glass spread across an inverted bowl of metal supports, and on the southernmost face a long entranceway extended forward, forming a covered platform. The railroad from the foothills below entered the construction through its open face and vanished within.

Outside, a group of horses shifted nervously, tugging at their reins and whining; their riders were already inside.

Targa walked with Duske and Dawne either side

17

of her, like a pair of watchful hounds trailing at her heels. The workers – there were few left up here now – scattered to get out of the trio's way when they approached, and any outriders nearby would either look away or tip their hat in respect. They were too afraid of her reputation to do any less.

They entered the vast atrium inside the dome, and while Targa's blindfolded face did not move an inch, both Duske and Dawne studied the construction around them, taking in every detail and sight of it. Where the tracks might have ended in an ordinary station, there was a set of sturdy buffers, but the metal rails continued on, into the dome proper. There, they were in the process of being connected to a pair of massive steel wells set into the tiled floor. Watching the operation, smiling like a well-fed predator, was the Master of it all, the architect of this place – Robur Drache.

Targa's hand quivered and she gingerly touched a finger to the cloth across her eyes, snatching it away when Drache glanced aside and noticed her. He beckoned her with a curled finger and she came quickly to him.

"Ahh, Targa," he breathed, savouring her name, "so good of you to make the trip up the mountain. Is this not my greatest work to date?"

She nodded slowly, her two bodyguards mimicking the movement. Drache gestured around with a rolled blueprint in one hand. "No common man

18

would have created such a thing as this, my dear. No ordinary person would have cause to." His face glowed with pride, the bald sheen of his head shaded to violet by the light entering the tinted dome. He adjusted the tiny pince-nez glasses on his nose, their obsidian lenses glittering as they caught the flames of a lamp. "But we are no ordinary people, are we?"

"Master Drache. I am always impressed by what I see."

Drache's face split in a feral smile. "What you *see*?" he said harshly. "What do you *see*, my dear?" He reached up his hand and brushed a trail of red hair from around the blindfold. Targa flinched, but held her ground. Drache shot a glare at Duske and Dawne. "Close your eyes, both of you. Now!"

The two women sighed as one and obeyed, and Targa wobbled a little.

"Now," Drache hissed quietly into her ear, "what do you see?"

Targa fought to control the fear in her voice. "Whatever you wish me to, my Master."

"Good!" Drache said, and snapped his fingers at Duske and Dawne, who blinked back at him. "Your understanding is always a joy to me, Targa. You have pleased me greatly in these last few months."

"It is my honour to serve," she said carefully.

"Yes, it is." Drache stepped closer to Dawne and smiled at her, showing a mouth full of silver teeth.

He stroked her hair gently. "You've done well keeping these people motivated, and for that I will reward you when our work here is done."

Drache parted Dawne's blonde tresses and examined a jewelled clasp set there with a detached, professional air. From a distance, it might have appeared to be a piece of ebony, but at close hand the decoration resembled a scarab beetle, held in place by a forest of tiny wires that wound around the woman's hair and vanished into the skin of her neck. Targa and Duske wore identical ornaments. Drache made a small sound of approval and stepped away, studying Targa carefully. His smile widened.

"I like you so much better now, darling Targa. You are obedient and loyal, without a dream of sedition in your beautiful head, correct?"

"Of course, Master Drache."

Drache nodded, and walked towards the centre of the dome, gesturing for the women to follow him. "Our recent impediments have been due to miscalculation on my part, you see. The abduction of the vassals from that dreary little town, what was it called?"

"Stonetree," Targa replied instantly.

"Ah, yes. Stonetree. I relied on Rook, and he failed me. We were unable to secure enough slaves and my schedule was put back. Then the mine, and that foolish Frenchman Trebuchet. He allowed ambition to outstrip his good sense and he died for it. That fool ruined my plans, he allowed those two meddling idiots to interfere in my affairs!" Drache checked his building anger with a grimace and licked his lips. "These were my errors. I know now that for my plans to succeed," he whirled around and spread his arms wide, "for our benefactor to be pleased, I must take a hand in things directly."

"The Indian and the gunslinger perished in the destruction of the Burnt Hills mine, Master," Targa said crisply. "I am sure of it."

"I hope for your sake you are right. To have them alive would have meant an extra reward from our benefactor, but their deaths still serve my purposes." He clapped his hands together. "Look here."

They stood in the exact middle of the glass hemisphere, on a wide disc of tile decorated with a green star six feet across; above, an identically-sized vent in the roof let the occasional flurry of snowflakes drift into the atrium. Duske and Dawne glanced around, noting the metal columns that hung down from the ceiling like stalactites, not quite touching the floor. Heavy cables wrapped in cloth connected the columns to each other and to the dome's framework, dangling like massive vines from some monstrous jungle tree.

"This endeavour is almost complete!" Drache's face was lit with anticipation and joy. "And once the last spike is hammered home, once the purpose of this place is fulfilled…" His voice trailed off into a whisper. "Then," he husked, "then the Long Night falls."

A scream cut through the air, and the four of them turned as one; a group of outriders were clustered around the tracks, hiding the source of the sound. Drache threw the blueprints aside and strode across the dome, his face thunderous. Targa and her guards followed, careful to stay out of his reach.

Drache shoved the outriders aside and sniffed. The air carried the stink of burnt skin. One of the men, a stocky outrider named Grover, had fallen into the shallow iron well and was struggling to clamber back out. Drache grabbed the nearest man and shook him. "You! Explain this!"

A former cavalry soldier busted out of the army, Ryder was one of the tallest outriders in Winterville, but he still shrank away from his master's anger. "He, he fell, ah, sir. Missed a step and just tumbled right in there."

Drache cast a cold glance down at Grover, then up at the dome roof. Above the wells, two large spars were suspended on oiled mechanisms, ready to drop down and slot into them with the throw of a knife-switch.

"Sir!" Grover cried, his eyes darting upward. "You're not gonna let them crush me, are ya?" The outrider slipped on the slick metal walls and coughed into his hands.

Drache shook his head. "Idiot. The time isn't right for that yet."

"Shouldn't we get him out?" Ryder ventured. "I'll get a rope."

Targa waved him away. "Get back to work," she snarled. Drache stepped back and nodded approvingly.

"But—" began Ryder.

"He's already dead," Targa growled. "Look again."

Ryder and the other men gingerly peeked over the lip of the well. Grover had changed; his hair was shoulder-length and white where it had been short and black only a second ago, a beard curled off his chin and his fingernails were long and crooked. Grover's coat and hat were disintegrating, falling apart before their eyes.

He croaked out a word. "Help..."

Ryder's mouth dropped open. "How'd he get so old? Like the life is being sucked out of him!"

"Still want to go in after him?" asked Targa.

The outriders backed away, and exchanged glances. "You heard the Governess!" Ryder said sharply. "Get back to work!"

Duske and Dawne craned their necks to study Grover's last moments. With a thin, wheezy wail, the unlucky outrider fell apart in a cloud of broken bones and dust, all that was left of him melting into the dark metal.

"I must remain here atop the mountain until all is ready." Drache nodded at Targa in a distracted fashion. "I am trusting you to maintain order in Winterville." He sighed. "Almost complete." The rail baron dropped into a crouch and ran a finger along the mouth of the well. "Not long now."

Targa and her guards stood and watched, silent and impassive.

It had taken all of Tyler's fast-talking skills to convince Fivehawk not to drop everything and walk up to the Black Train, barefaced and as bold as you like, demanding to call out Drache himself. The irony of it was not lost on the cowboy; typically, *he* was the one with the hot head and zero self-control.

Fivehawk accepted grudgingly, and the two men had taken the back way out of the inn, wary that Drache's outriders might be lurking on the main street. Within moments, they had recovered their horses and stolen away towards the edge of town, where the buildings parted way for the foothills of Frost Peak.

Tyler didn't want to be the one to say it, but he did anyway. "Listen, Jonathan. We gotta play this cool ... I mean, just 'cause Drache's steam engine is in town don't mean that your sister is there too…"

The Indian opened his mouth to protest and then caught himself. "You are right. For a change." He paused, thinking. "We cannot reveal ourselves just yet. We need to scout the area and locate Drache."

"Yeah." Tyler nodded. "He might just be passing through, or something."

Fivehawk shook his head. "No. I should have known when I saw those Chinese outside the town. Where there is hardship and human misery, the influence of The Faceless is never far from hand."

Tyler's eyes narrowed but he said nothing, and Fivehawk gave him a hard stare in return. "What is it, Paleface? After all this time, you still doubt that the demon is as real as you or I?"

"Well, I…" Tyler fumbled. "It's just that it is a little tough for me to get my head around the idea of a monster from the sky riding a big magic rock, is all…"

Fivehawk's face creased in annoyance and he spurred on his horse, leaving Tyler behind.

"Fivehawk, wait!" the cowboy called. "I'm supposed to be the impulsive one, remember?"

An uncomfortable silence lay between them as they picked their way up into the timberline on the mountain's flank. Once in a while, Fivehawk would glance out at the foothills and catch a glimpse of woodland, sometimes a bright snake of railroad tracks peeking though the ever-present mist. The ground here was thick with snow, and it crunched quietly beneath their horses' hooves. Behind him, Tyler sniffed and rubbed his gloved hands together for warmth.

The Indian halted his mount and jumped down from the saddle in a single swift move. Tyler's hand dropped to the butt of his Springfield rifle, protruding from its saddle holster. "Trouble?"

Fivehawk cocked his head and sank to his haunches. "Perhaps. There are tracks here, fresh ones."

Warily, Tyler dismounted and opened his long coat, so he could draw his six-gun if need arose. "Show me."

"Look." Fivehawk pointed out a trail of depressions in the snow, canine footprints with unusual claw marks. "Guardians, I have no doubt of it."

"Guardians? Like those mastiff dogs we tangled with in Stonetree? But those prints look more like wolves." Tyler's face wrinkled as he remembered the rotten-meat stench of the animals, their yellowed, wicked teeth.

Fivehawk nodded. "The beasts have many shapes. The Faceless takes the animals that live and turns them to Its will. We shall find Guardian wolves here."

"Great," said Tyler, turning on the spot to survey the area. He paused; from where they stood, the valley was almost level with them and the thin fog that shrouded it seemed like a disc of cotton wool. His brow furrowed. "You know what I don't get about all this? Why the heck is Drache building a railroad way up here in Frozen-Backside? We gotta be hundreds of miles off the beaten track, nowhere near the North-Western lines ... I mean, why would anyone want to come way out here?"

"I care not about his motives. You know why we have come."

"Yeah, your sister. Eyes-Like-Amber, right?"

Fivehawk tried to conceal his reaction to her name and failed. "Drache would not build an iron road for nothing. He took the people of Stonetree to be his slaves, he mined the Burnt Hills for the sky rock ... he does nothing without a reason."

"True," Tyler allowed. "If we can figure out what that reason is, we could use it against—"

A twig broke with a sharp crack above their heads, and both men whirled to look up. Fivehawk caught a flash of colour in the branches of a tree before something dived at him in a blur of movement.

For a split-second, Tyler hesitated as his mind filled up with images of huge wolves with eyes like red embers, and then the attacker was on the Indian, crashing into him and barrelling Fivehawk over. It was a human figure, swaddled in rags and cloth strips against the cold, with a bandage-concealed head that reminded him of an Egyptian mummy.

Fivehawk felt all the air leave his lungs in a painful whoosh as his assailant landed feet-first on his torso; dazed, he tumbled and rolled into a heap, wheezing. The raggedy figure turned on its heel and sprang at Tyler like a cat. The cowboy's hand flashed towards his gun and drew the weapon, but he was a heartbeat too slow – Raggedy's arms spun up at him like sword blades and connected with his pistol arm and his chin, sending his Peacemaker up and out of his grip. The impact was enough to set the weapon off, and a single shot broke through the cold air like thunder. Tyler stumbled back a step and swayed, fighting to keep his balance – perhaps they'd been caught unawares by this dirt-bag, but he wasn't about to roll over nice and easy for him. The cowboy shook off the pain in his arms and raised his fists, boxer style.

"Put up your dukes, Rag-man! Let's have at it!"

Then Raggedy did something Tyler had never seen before in a hundred different fistfights and punch-ups: he pivoted on a heel like a can-can dancer and brought his other leg up in a spinning kick. Tyler tried to block it and missed by a country mile. The canvas sole of Raggedy's shoe connected with his temple and he twisted away, dropping like a felled tree with bright lights exploding inside his skull.

Fivehawk was back on his feet by now, and he shrugged off his long coat as the attacker turned back to face him. From a pocket in his buckskin jacket, the Indian drew the stubby shape of a tomahawk and spun it around his hand. He advanced, eyes never leaving his foe. Raggedy's expression was invisible behind his shroud of cloth, but Fivehawk swore he could see the glitter of sharp eyes behind two rough rips in the mask. He seemed to nod to himself, and then his hand darted into a pocket and emerged again with a length of pole, no longer than Fivehawk's forearm. Raggedy flicked it and it fell open to twice its length – there were actually two poles, connected to each other by a short span of chain. The Indian had a split second to wonder over the manner of this weapon before Raggedy flicked it up and spun it around his head, over his arms and out, twirling the end so it spun like a windmill.

Fivehawk kicked at a clump of snow by his feet, and flicked it into the air; at the same moment, he lunged with his axe and slashed downward. Raggedy blocked with his weapon and the blade sang as it glanced off the spinning pole. Fivehawk tried again and cried out as the weapon cracked across his knuckles. Still, he held the tomahawk firmly, and cut outward, across the attacker's chest. The lip of the axe blade sheared through a quarter-inch of the cloth on Raggedy's chest, making some of it drop away into the snow. He replied with a hit on Fivehawk's chin that staggered him backward, and then Raggedy moved in to deliver the *coup de grâce*. The Indian saw it coming and brought up the tomahawk.

Raggedy flipped the weapon over into an X-shape, and the chain met the axehead with a flash of sparks; suddenly Fivehawk and the cloth-wrapped assailant were locked in a test of strength.

A well-oiled click gave them both a moment's pause. Staggering to his feet, his recovered Peacemaker in his hand, Tyler aimed the pistol carefully at the fighters.

He wobbled slightly, the foot-in-the-head still having robbed him of some balance.

"OK, playtime is over, Rag-man. Why don't you reach for the sky and drop that ... uh, whatever it is?"

"Tyler!" Fivehawk hissed. "Miss and you'll hit me!"

The cowboy blinked. "Oh, p'shaw. I can shoot the wings off a fly at two hundred yards, so plugging this guy right between the eyes will be a piece of cake."

If Raggedy understood, their attacker gave no sign; but then Fivehawk felt the tension relax and the figure stepped away, still holding the pole-chain weapon, ignoring Tyler's demands.

The Indian studied him for a moment. "He kicks like a mule ... but he doesn't smell like one. Whoever this is, he's not one of Drache's outriders."

"Holy Cats, you mean we got another set of bad guys to be worried about? We gotta beat the outriders and a bunch of tree-hiding snow mummies?"

"You fight outriders?" A muffled voice emerged from the bandaged figure.

"We do," Fivehawk said warily. "Are you their ally?"

Raggedy's body tensed. "No! I am revenge! I am the living storm that will wipe them off the face of this mountain!" The smothered voice was angry and sharp.

"Then we should not fight. Our path is one shared." The Indian put away his tomahawk and spread his hands in a gesture of peace. "I am Fivehawk, a wanderer of the Ulanutani tribe. The paleface is Tyler."

"Pleased to meet ya," Gabriel interjected, holding the gun steady.

Raggedy pocketed the weapon and reached up, unwinding the cloth strips. They fell away to reveal a shock of unkempt, shoulder-length black hair and a pale, golden face with almond-shaped eyes. "My name is Yu Lim."

"A woman!" Fivehawk said in surprise.

Tyler dropped his pistol back into the holster. "Yeah, and let's not forget, a woman who just kicked us up and down the mountain."

Fivehawk opened his mouth to speak, but a distant sound came to his ears: the baying of wolves. "Guardians," he hissed.

"What?" Tyler's eyes darted around. "Now?"

"Perhaps word of our arrival spread faster than we

thought. We must find a place to conceal ourselves, or else they will trap us up here."

"But what about the horses? We can't just leave them to be found..."

"I know a place," Yu Lim interrupted. "A cave, not far from here."

The two men exchanged glances. "Can we trust her?" Tyler asked.

The sounds of the wolves were closer now, and there were the rough-voiced shouts of men among them.

"Do you have a better idea?"

Tyler scowled then gestured to the Chinese girl. "Well, then. Lead on, miss."

3: AN UNCOMMON ENEMY

"Intruders," growled Targa, as the sound of the gunshot reached her ears. She pulled her horse to a halt and stabbed a finger at Heller. "No one is allowed on the mountain without my permission – who would be shooting off a weapon here?"

The outrider chewed his lip, glancing at Duske and Dawne, who both stared levelly back at him. "Uh, nobody, ma'am. Like you say, the Winterville folks know that it's more than their lives are worth to go poking around up here."

"I won't tolerate disobedience!" she hissed, nodding to Dawne. "Can you see them?"

Dawne reached into her jacket and removed a compact set of spyglasses, like two stubby telescopes connected together. Another of Master Drache's mysterious "gifts", the lenses were very powerful, and a tiny switch on the grip of the device turned a normal view into a complex pattern of colours, where cool blue indicated the cold landscape and hot orange betrayed the heat of living creatures. "Searching…" Dawne mumbled, her head tracking from east to west.

Heller nodded to Mantooth, the other outrider in their group. A rat-faced figure with a single, over-long canine forever poking out of his mouth, he was a quiet and watchful thug. Mantooth pursed his lips and gave a low whistle; within moments, a quartet of grey wolves emerged from the shadows of the tree line, panting and sniffing the air. The animals halted at the feet of the outrider's horse and glanced up at him. Each of the dogs had fur the colour of charcoal, and eyes that blazed with a baleful inner fire.

"We'll bag them," Heller was saying. "Smell 'em out and catch them real good."

Dawne's enhanced gaze swept over the flanks of the mountain, and suddenly a speckle of shapes leapt out at her. She adjusted a dial on the spyglasses and the fuzzy image sharpened; horses, three figures. One swaddled in rags, one hidden under a hat, the other dark-haired and bare-headed...

Targa's breath came out in a gasp. "It can't be! Look closer!"

Dawne turned the dial a little more and the faces of the two men filled her vision. She twitched, and Duske mimicked her, as Targa swore out loud and spat into the snow.

"They live!" she snarled, her teeth showing like an animal's. "They should be buried under a thousand tons of rock and yet they live! Curse them both!"

"Who are these men?" Dawne asked.

"The gunslinger and the Indian." Targa bit out each word, as if saying them gave her pain to do so. "Why aren't they dead?"

Duske shivered and raised a hand to her temple, as if to rub away an ache. "Governess, you spoke of these two as if they had been destroyed—"

"I know what I said!" Targa's voice rose an octave. "They have more lives than a cat!"

"There is another with them," Dawne said. "I cannot see a face…"

"I don't care!" she turned to Heller. "Get down there and kill them! Kill them and bring their heads to me, now!"

Heller blinked. "But Master Drache will want to know—"

Targa's hand flew up and slapped Heller hard across the face. "Don't question me! Take the Guardians and tear those fools limb from limb!"

Mantooth click-clicked his tongue against his teeth and the wolves tensed. Heller rubbed at his face and nodded. "Of course, ma'am."

With the pack of dogs running at their heels, Heller and Mantooth rode away at a fast clip, kicking up puffs of snow.

Dawne hesitated, then spoke. "Master Drache will be displeased if we keep news of these intruders from him."

Targa gave a short, harsh laugh. "He has his plans

to occupy him. The first he shall know of them is when I hand him their heads on a lance!" Her hands gingerly reached to her face, gently caressing the blindfold over her eyes. *And then*, she added silently, *our benefactor might see fit to release me from Drache's constant torment...*

Tyler pulled Yu Lim up into his saddle just as Fivehawk's cry reached their ears. "Here they come!"

The two outriders swept down through the trees towards them, with four wolves racing alongside. Yu Lim felt Tyler's body go tense as he spied the animals. "What are they?" she asked.

"They're no ordinary dogs, you can be sure of that!"

Fivehawk pumped a round into his rifle and fired, the shot impacting the snow just ahead of the wolves, but the creatures came on, jaws wide and slavering.

"To the ridge!" Yu Lim cried out. "Quickly!"

Tyler and Fivehawk urged their mounts into a gallop and they thundered across the frosty clearing and into the sparse timberline. Frost-rimed trees flashed past them, thin branches snapping off in the wake of their headlong passage.

There was a crack behind them and a bullet whined past Tyler's ear, making him duck sharply. Fivehawk slipped his rifle back into its holster and dropped back, letting Tyler pass him.

"What are you doing?" the cowboy asked. "Keep up, man!"

"I'm going to even the odds!" Fivehawk cast a quick glance over his shoulder, and then made a play of turning his mount left, then right, then left again. Sure enough, one of the outriders caught sight of him and followed, leaving the other to chase Tyler. Acting quickly, Fivehawk slowed to a trot and glanced around, searching for a suitable tree. He gave a small smile when he found just what he was looking for.

Heller rode his mount between the tightly packed trunks with one hand, the other gripping his .44 calibre revolver, the hammer cocked and ready to fire. He licked his lips and grimaced. It was typical of that high-and-mighty redhead harpy to make him risk his neck instead of her precious bodyguards. He brushed the thought away with a snarl. *No matter*, he thought. Just one shot in that redskin's back, or a bullet in his horse's flank,would bring Heller's target down and let the wolves take their pleasure with him.

His face froze as he spotted Fivehawk just ahead, stock-still and inviting him to fire. *This is too easy...* Heller's finger tightened on the trigger; but with his attention on the shot he was a split-second too late to realize that Fivehawk was gripping a length of tree branch in his hand.

He released the branch as Heller came within

37

reach, and the six-foot-long bough of wood, still connected to its parent trunk, sprang from where Fivehawk had bent it back along its length. The branch connected with Heller's chest and the outrider flew backwards out of his saddle and into a crumpled heap in the snow, quite literally out cold. His riderless mount careened away, out of control.

Fivehawk nodded, pleased with his handiwork. As he paused, rough howls and loud shouts came to him – Tyler and the girl were still in trouble! The Indian tugged on his reins and set his horse into a gallop.

Yu Lim kicked one of the wolves in the snout as it leapt up to snap at her ankle, her face wrinkled with disgust. "What are these *guei lang* monsters?"

"What you say?" Tyler said, over the rush of wind.

"Demon wolf. That is what these beasts are."

Another gunshot splintered a tree as they raced past it, showering them with snowflakes. "Ah, I've had about enough of this guy." Tyler growled. "Miss? Hold these!" He handed Yu Lim the reins, and the startled Chinese girl grabbed at them.

"What are you doing?" she asked, wide-eyed.

Tyler drew his gun and turned around in his saddle, twisting at his waist and leaning out to the left. "Time for a little patented Tyler trick-shot!" He cocked the gun and drew a careful bead on Mantooth.

"You are mad!"

"That's for sure." Tyler blew out a breath and fired.

Their pursuer gawked as he suddenly realized the purpose of Tyler's horseback gymnastics, and he dug his spurs into his mount's flank – a second too late. Tyler's Peacemaker spat out a single .45 round that impacted squarely in the middle of the outrider's kneecap, shattering the bone as it passed through. A fan of greenish-red blood jetted into the air, and Mantooth gave a gurgling scream. Pulling at his horse, the outrider turned it off its hooves and down on to the wet earth. The animal landed directly on top of him with a panicked screech.

Yu Lim smiled, impressed with Tyler's accuracy. "Amazing! You *are* a good marksman, after all."

Tyler grunted as he pulled himself back up into the saddle. "Not really. I was aiming for his head."

The Guardian wolves faltered and fell behind, pausing to sniff at Mantooth, unsure about proceeding without him. Barely conscious, he hissed out a high-pitched peep from between clenched teeth and sent the dogs, their needle-sharp fangs bared and bright red tongues lolling, racing after their prey once more.

Tyler's horse burst out of the tree line and into an open clearing, blocked on three sides by a sheer rock face. Fivehawk was waiting for them, his rifle cradled in his arms.

Tyler cursed loudly. "We took a wrong turn!"

"No, this is the right place," Yu Lim countered, dropping down from the saddle. "I came up from the crevasse below through here."

"There's no cave here," Fivehawk began. "Just rock and—"

"Snow!" she said with a grin, and pushed at a section of the rock face.

It was Tyler's turn for surprise when the girl fell *into* the wall. "Ah, no," he said with feeling. "Not another one of those hidden caves!"

Closer, and they could see where Yu Lim had disappeared. A fallen tree, concealed by the snow, had collapsed with its branches across a cavern entrance, and the following snowfalls had formed a cover over it. Dropping out of the saddle, Fivehawk took the reins of his horse and lead the skittish animal inside, then did the same for Tyler.

The cowboy and the Indian exchanged nervous glances; the wolves were coming back, their yelps getting closer by the second.

"They have our scent," Fivehawk said flatly.

Tyler checked his pistol, quickly replacing the spent cartridges with fresh ones. "Right. I reckon our best chance is to pick them off as they come for us."

Yu Lim emerged from the darkness. "Those demons are too fast. Kill one and the next will be sinking his teeth into your throat before you can draw breath."

Fivehawk glanced quickly out at the tree line, then back to the girl. "You have something else in mind?"

She pointed into the darkness of the cave. "There is another way into this cavern. That is how I found it. It leads down to the valley. We can get the horses out there."

"Doesn't stop the wolves coming after us, though," Tyler added. He could hear the dogs padding through the bushes now, and could see branches shifting as they came closer. They had slowed; now they were hunting the three humans.

"I grew up in the mountains in China," Yu Lim said, taking in a deep lungful of air, "and one thing I will never forget is how dangerous snow can be."

"Pardon?" Tyler began. "Is that one of them Chinese proverbs?"

Fivehawk's face fell as understanding struck him. "Quick, get inside!" He grabbed Tyler's arm and pulled him deeper into the cave.

"What? What's she going to do?"

The wolves emerged from the trees and came to a halt, snarling and sniffing the air. The biggest of the group swung his pointed snout around and spotted Yu Lim. Her voice almost died in her throat when she realized he was the very beast she'd kicked off her only moments ago. She saw an almost human glimmer of anger in his flame-coloured eyes and then the wolf came at her, the other three a half-step behind.

Yu Lim opened her mouth … and sang.

Tyler's eyes bugged. The Chinese girl let out a strong, piercing note from the top of the register and held it for agonizingly long second – and then, as if in answer, the mountain itself grumbled and trembled around them.

Rivers of fresh snow began to slide down the rock face; there was a moment's pause, and then a huge mass of white shifted off the mountainside and down into the clearing. The Guardian wolves yelped and skidded, turning about in panic even as the avalanche bore down on them. The lead dog howled and snapped at the snowfall, crying out in fury once before the giant weight smothered his pack.

It was a while before a dazed and bruised Heller cantered into the clearing in search of the beasts. There was no sign, no evidence of them or their quarry or Yu Lim's cave, had he known to look for the latter. The outrider shuddered in the wintry silence; not because of the cold, but in fear of the Governess Targa. She would not be pleased. He moved off in search of Mantooth; perhaps, if he were dead, Heller could blame the failure on him instead…

Deep inside the cave, the darkness was absolute, and Fivehawk took care to stroke the flanks of his nervous mount as he fished blindly for the tinderbox in his saddlebags. "Here," he said, passing it by touch to Tyler. "There are matches inside."

The gunslinger struck a light and touched it to a lamp wick, and the cave suddenly came alive with dancing flickers of flame. The walls were slippery and water-worn, dripping with melted ice.

Tyler pushed away thoughts of another cave and turned to Yu Lim. "So, how'd you learn to do that, uh, singing thing?"

"The Peking Opera," she replied curtly.

"Oh. Right." Tyler nodded, none the wiser.

The girl smiled and both Fivehawk and Tyler realized for the first time that beneath her dirt-streaked face, Yu Lim was quite an exotic beauty. The trio ventured still further into the mountain, until they stopped to rest in a wide chamber. A vent in the wall opened out on to another part of the mountainside, a shaded crevasse with steep, almost sheer walls.

"You took a big risk out there," Fivehawk said. "How did you know that you'd start an avalanche here?"

"I trust in Heaven," she said simply. "My Ancestors will not let me die until my duty is fulfilled."

Tyler gave Fivehawk a sideways look. "And what duty would that be, exactly?"

Yu Lim's face hardened, and she glanced out into the fading daylight, her smile vanishing as if it had never been there. "Night will fall soon. I would ask if I may have a rope from one of you."

"What for?" asked Fivehawk.

"I must climb the mountain."

"Alone?" Tyler was incredulous. "If you don't freeze to death in those pyjamas you are wearing, the outriders will be sure to shoot you soon as look at you."

"This will not happen to me."

The cowboy continued. "You can bet there are more of 'em, and probably plenty more of those wolves, too."

"I can take care of myself!" Yu Lim snapped. "Or did you forget how I knocked you down with just my dainty, girlish foot?"

Tyler's mouth opened and closed, and he threw up his hands in frustration, looking to Fivehawk. "She's a stubborn as a mule!"

"Yes. Remind you of anyone?" the Indian said dryly.

"Hey," scowled Tyler, "you're supposed to be on my side, remember?"

Fivehawk nodded to himself, and met Yu Lim's cold glare evenly. "I wonder if we might all be on the same side. Tyler and I are here in search of someone – you spoke before of your duty, of revenge against the outriders."

"Do not stand in my way." Yu Lim's eyes glittered in the lamplight.

"I have no intention of doing that … but perhaps we might be able to help each other along the way."

Tyler nodded. "Three instead of two. Or, uh, one, in your case. Makes better odds in the long run, I guess."

"We have no debts to each other," Yu Lim said carefully. "We pooled our skills to escape the wolves and that is that. Why should I accept your help? You cannot know the obligation I must fulfil."

Fivehawk's head bobbed in agreement. "You may think so. Now let me convince you otherwise." The Indian dipped his fingers into the leather-bound medicine bundle that hung around his neck on a lanyard. With a flick of his wrist, he tossed a pinch of powder into the lamp flame and it grew to twice its previous size. Yu Lim started, and Tyler blinked in surprise.

"When Tyler and I met, it was not an accident. Our paths crossed because of the will of the Great Spirit, what he would call God…"

"The will of Heaven." Yu Lim's eyes were drawn to the flames; in amongst the leaping colours, shapes and forms danced, changing and shifting.

"The name you give it is not important," Fivehawk said with a nod. "We came together, both searching for the blood of our blood, to a place that had the life stolen from it."

"It was a ghost town," Tyler broke in suddenly, speaking aloud before even he was aware of the reason why. "A whole town of people, gone. My uncle was one of them, and Fivehawk, well, his sister had already been taken…" The cowboy's words drifted into silence as he too became entranced by the firelight. *Strange how the mind plays tricks on you*, he thought, *I could swear I saw a face in there.*

Fivehawk spoke again. "This man who walks with demons, eyes hidden behind panes of darkness, he was the master of this malignancy. We followed the trail into the deep desert to find this Drache, but we only succeeded in destroying one of his slave camps and freeing his prisoners."

"But this Drache … he is like an evil dream, something released from one of the many hells," breathed Yu Lim. "I know it in my heart. No man could inflict the cruelty I have seen my people suffer here, no man could do that and stay human."

Fivehawk leant forward. "My people have a legend, of a creature called The Faceless, a dark spirit of corruption…"

"He reckons this rattlesnake Drache is in league with it," Tyler said. "He's a filthy jasper and no mistake, with a line of black deeds behind him as wide as the Rockies…" The cowboy shook his head to clear it of the heavy, hypnotic air in the cave, and eyed the other man. "Listen to this mumbo-jumbo. Anybody listening to us would think we're all crazy."

Fivehawk studied Yu Lim and saw encouragement in her eyes. "Perhaps. Or perhaps not."

"You're buying this?" Tyler said to her, half-heartedly. "Heck, I've been listening to his boojum stories for weeks now and I'm just plain confused by the whole darn thing."

"Tyler thinks that to believe is to show weakness," said Fivehawk. "What do you believe, Yu Lim?"

The Chinese girl stood up and walked to the cave mouth. "Even if I had no trust in Heaven and no kind thoughts for my Ancestors, I would still believe this Drache is a monster in human skin. Look here." She pointed out into the snow.

Tyler and Fivehawk followed her gesture to the floor of the crevasse. What they had both seen from the corner of their eyes and dismissed as broken scraps of a fallen tree was now clear to them. Here and there, sticking out from the blanket of snow, were the hands of frozen corpses. The canyon was choked with them, a silent, icy mass grave.

"Oh dear Lord," Tyler breathed.

Yu Lim stared up into the darkening sky. When she spoke again, the certainty in her voice was cold as the ice surrounding them. "Even if I had no belief, I have enough vengeance in me to kill a thousand monsters."

4: DEATH TRAP

Targa's half-hidden face was neutral as she sipped at a glass of wine; everything about her manner was languid and relaxed as she sat in the heavy leather chair facing the roaring fireplace. She replaced the glass on a tray that Duske held by her side and gave an imperceptible nod to Dawne, who stood close by. "Go on, Heller."

The outrider shot a hard glance at Mantooth, who was leaning heavily against another, empty chair. "Well, it's like this…" Heller mumbled, kneading the brim of his doffed hat. "We got separated, see. The Indian, he blindsided me and when I got back in the saddle … well, Mantooth had lost them."

Mantooth shook his head. "Ain't so!" His protruding canine tooth made his words come out in hisses and whistles. "I took a bullet! I sent the wolves right after 'em. Ain't no way they would escape." The outrider balanced awkwardly on one leg, his injured knee set with a rough splint and tied with a dirty bandage.

Targa shook her head slowly, the first flare of

irritation making a nerve jump in her jaw. "As the Governess of this town, I have certain responsibilities," she began. "This mansion is the symbol of them." Targa gestured around at the walls of the ornate room around them. It was a dark place, made of mahogany panels that were deep red, lit by a trio of gas lamps and the hearth's dancing flames. "People in Winterville look at this place and they know that I'm watching them. All of them." She pointed out of the window. "Look out there, Heller. What do you see?"

Heller took a cautious step towards the glass. "The garden?"

"The garden," Targa repeated with a nod. "In many ways, what I do for Master Drache is what a gardener does."

Dawne walked slowly to a bookshelf on the far wall, and ran her finger along the volumes, searching for a particular one. Heller glanced to her, then back to Targa.

The Governess nodded to the injured outrider. "Sit, Mantooth, sit. You'll never heal if you stay on your feet." Mantooth obeyed, failing to conceal the fear in his eyes.

Targa turned back to face Heller. He had the sense that, even though her eyes were covered, she was still staring back at him. "I pluck the troublesome plants from the garden," she continued, "and you are my tools. But if I miss a weed here or

49

there, then soon all the precious blooms are strangled, are they not?"

Heller's mouth worked but no sound emerged. "They gotta be dead, ma'am!" He managed. "There was an avalanche … there's gotta be a hundred ton of snow—"

Targa held up a hand to silence him. "Weeds are hardy. Unless you pull them up by the roots, they live on. A blunt blade that will not cut them out is of no use to me. Understand, Heller?"

"It was his fault!" Heller's voice broke, and he stabbed a finger at Mantooth. "His dumb dogs let them get away!"

"Yes," said Targa, nodding to Dawne, "they did."

Dawne pulled at a copy of *Journey to the Centre of the Earth* and a switch behind the bookcase gave a soft click. Mantooth's chair and a section of the floor it sat on suddenly tilted forward and the outrider fell into a dark trapdoor that opened beneath him. His strangled yelp was cut off as the now-empty chair righted itself and returned to its place.

Heller jumped at the sight, his heart in his mouth. "Wh-where did he go?"

In answer, Duske reached over to a candlestick on the hearth's mantelpiece and gave it a quarter-turn. Above the fireplace, an unpleasantly lifelike portrait of Robur Drache retracted to reveal a strange map: a maze-like model of a series of rooms, each connected to the other by a corridor. Heller stepped closer for a better look and saw that a bright silver ball had dropped into the first of these.

Mantooth cried out as he hit the floor, falling in a heap from the slide that deposited him in the empty wooden cell. Dragging himself up, he looked around at his new surroundings. There were no doors or windows, only a lamp hanging by a hook on one wall, and the hatch he had dropped through. The outrider reached up to it, hoping he might be able to haul himself back up, but a panel slid down and closed it. He cursed, and grabbed at the lamp; as he did, a door opened in one of the walls.

The outrider saw an empty room and began to cross it, gingerly waving his arms in front of him in case something were to leap out. Something brushed at his right hand, plucking at his fingers. Mantooth brought his palm up to his face and screeched in pain and realization – his thumb and forefinger were gone, sliced away. In the lamplight he caught a flicker of reflection from a net of fine, razor-sharp wires, invisible to the naked eye. He had almost blundered into them. Mantooth curled his injured hand in a claw and stumbled forward, through the next door. *How many of these traps are there?* he wondered. How long would he have to stay here before he was released from this maze of death?

Targa clapped her hands. "Ha! Score one for him."

The silver ball fell again. The next room had a swirl of green decorating it. Heller glanced at the Governess, who held a finger to her lips. "He's put on a good show, but this will be an end to him."

The smell hit Mantooth first, just as his good foot touched the floor and sank down to his ankle. He stumbled and fell over, the lamp dropping out of his grasp. Where his uninjured hand touched the spongy floor, thick mossy syrup clung to it, setting the skin afire. The outrider shook off the fumes that filled his nose and mouth, coughing for air. Quicklime! The room was filled with a mattress of the deadly chemical, and it burnt and cut into his soft skin. With a bestial roar Mantooth collapsed into it and shouted a final, wordless curse at Targa.

From somewhere deep in the lower floors of the mansion, a long, hollow thud sounded, and, as Heller watched, the silver ball disappeared back into the map's mechanism. Duske twisted the candlestick back into place, and Drache's fearsome visage returned to its watchful position. He eyed the chair where Mantooth had sat as a man might watch a cobra with flared hood and bared fangs.

Targa took another sip of wine. "Get Ryder, Grizzly and the others. Take the Guardians if you have to, but find me those two men, and whoever that was with them. Find them and destroy them!"

Heller nodded, and stuttered his thanks. It dawned on him that he'd been spared despite his mistake … but now he would have to make good on it.

"They never left the mountain." Targa purred. "I want you to bring them to me before Master Drache even knows they were there, understand?"

"I'll find them, ma'am. You can count on it."

"Good. Because if you don't, then we'll see how far you get through the maze before you die."

Night descended on Frost Peak like the fall of a vast, silent curtain, bringing with it a light flurry of snow. Fivehawk sniffed the air as his horse emerged from the crevasse, out on to the main mountain trail. Behind him, Yu Lim shifted uncomfortably and held on to his saddle. Tyler followed, and the cowboy's face spoke volumes; all three of them were glad to get out of the icy gorge, with its population of corpses worked to death by Drache's outriders.

Fivehawk watched the sky for a moment. "There is a storm on the way."

"Then we should waste no time," Yu Lim said. "We can use the cover of night to reach the summit unseen."

"It's never that easy…" murmured Tyler, checking his Peacemaker before returning it to his holster.

The Indian gave him an arch look. "When have you ever known us to have an easy day?"

53

A rueful smile creased Tyler's face. "I suppose not."

They rode in silence, the slow, steady snowfall casting a blanket of quiet over the whole landscape. *Strange*, mused Fivehawk, *how these flakes remind me of winters as a child, clustered around campfires with Father's stories, and Eyes-Like-Amber beside me*... He shook his head to clear it of the reverie.

"What is wrong?" asked Yu Lim softly.

"My sister," said the Indian, infusing those two simple words with all the longing and sadness he felt inside.

The woman nodded. "I understand."

"Hey!" hissed Tyler. "Up ahead! What's that?"

Fivehawk looked and saw what appeared to be a barn, built on the very edge of the trail so that a good quarter of the wooden shack was hanging out over the valley. As they drew closer, he noticed a few ropes that seemed to extend out of the barn and out into the mist over the ravine.

"It is one of Drache's constructions," Yu Lim explained as they approached, "there is a pulley inside that hauls a platform up and down from the valley floor."

"Why is it here?" Fivehawk looked around. "There is no camp here, no buildings."

"Not now." She pointed up, to the mountain peak. "When the workers were first brought here, they were made to build this so Drache could bring great

54

steel beams and panes of glass up the mountain without horses or wagons. Whatever he made from them is there, at the pinnacle." The girl paused. "He is there also. He never leaves the peak."

They pulled level with the barn; the frost-covered shack was inert and dark. Tyler twitched and drew his gun. "Something ain't right here."

"What do you mean?"

"I mean, I gotta bad feeling about this."

Yu Lim made a face. "It is nothing but an empty barn—"

As if her words had been the trigger, the snow beneath them erupted as a concealed length of cable was pulled tight. Caught under their horses' hooves, the thick cord pulled at the legs of their mounts and put them off-balance.

"It's an ambush!" Tyler swore as his brown-and-white mare wickered and tumbled, throwing him off into a heap. Fivehawk and Yu Lim fared no better, the girl falling into a snowdrift and the Indian collapsing to his hands and knees. In the next second, gunfire erupted from the bushes.

"Scatter!" yelled Tyler, scrambling to his feet. He cast a quick look over his shoulder and was rewarded by the sight of his companions doing just that, then brought up his gun and fired at the muzzle flashes.

Fivehawk turned as a familiar yowl filled his ears. Two grey wolves bolted out of the darkness towards him, two pairs of blood-hungry eyes aglow with hatred. His bow and quiver were to one side, too awkward to reach. He brought up his arm to protect his throat just as the first beast leapt at him and sank inch-long fangs into his forearm. Biting back the pain, the Indian drew his buck knife as the second wolf pounced. This predator was not so lucky, and Fivehawk's blade sank into its flank. The other beast gnawed and tore at his arm, soaking the sleeve of his buckskin jacket with saliva and blood.

"Rush 'em!"

Tyler heard Heller's shouted order and drew a bead as the outrider bolted from cover carrying a rifle. Ryder, a drawn cavalry sabre in his hands, followed behind, and the huge man-mountain shape of Grizzly came last. The hair-covered outrider saw Tyler and bellowed like his bear namesake, thundering across the snow towards him. The cowboy's pistol turned and fired twice, then snapped as the hammer fell again on an empty chamber. Two bullets struck Grizzly square in the chest, but the huge man shrugged them off like bee stings. Tyler flipped the gun around his fingers and hit the outrider with it as he came within arm's reach. He might as well have struck with a snowball for all the effect it made; Grizzly crashed into him and brought Tyler to the ground with a numbing impact. Gabriel choked as the big man rested a meaty hand over his throat, the air in his lungs fading and the blood rushing through his ears.

Yu Lim saw the glint in Ryder's eyes as he came for her, swinging the blade of his sabre before him in an arc that flashed with moonlight.

"I'll cut the fight right outta you!" he hissed, showing brown-stained teeth.

She held back a smile and fell into a fighting stance, her left hand reaching into her jacket and returning with a long, cloth-wrapped object.

"What you got there, Chinee girl? A big ol' stick to hit Mister Ryder with?"

Flicking her wrist, Yu Lim jerked away the cloth cover to reveal a leather scabbard; with the grace born from thousands of days of practice, she pulled at one end and drew a flat-bladed short sword. Her face split in a grin and she beckoned Ryder closer.

The outrider felt a twitch of pain dart through his head like a knife. The sword had less reach than his, but the blade ... the blade was not metal, but some kind of strange stone-like material – it was jade, a creamy blue-green, and it glowed in the twilight. Ryder's expression hardened. No matter. He would chop off her hand, and then the problem would be solved.

Fivehawk fought to part the wolf's jaws from his arm, but the beast held on. With a great effort, he clutched at his medicine bundle and squeezed it; a puff of powder emerged and the animal's eyes widened. It sniffed – and then sneezed, releasing him.

"What the heck?" Heller was close, his rifle ready to shoot. "You damn stupid mutt!" he shouted at the dog. "Bite him!"

Fivehawk took the opportunity and bodily threw the wolf in Heller's direction. The outrider cried out, dropping his weapon as the creature landed on him. The Indian dived for cover, shouldering open the doors to the barn and ducking inside. Fivehawk hesitated a moment, face wrinkling in pain at the wounds the Guardian wolf had inflicted.

A window shattered as a rifle round crashed through it. Outside, he heard Heller's rough laughter and the click-click of a tinderbox being struck.

Tyler brought up his hands and clapped Grizzly hard over the ears as his vision began to tunnel, but the shaggy monster simply shrugged it off and kept up the pressure. The cowboy's thoughts became sluggish and foggy; his gun was empty, punches and kicks didn't seem to work. It was as if this hairy ape had absolutely no soft spots at all…

Soft spot. Tyler's brain said. *Every man's gotta soft spot.*

Marshalling the last of his strength, Tyler put all his effort into one last attack and brought up his knee as hard as he could between Grizzly's legs. He was rewarded with a hollow grunt from his attacker, and the huge outrider's eyes crossed in agony. Grizzly fell into a heap in the snow and curled up in a ball, with a thin squeal escaping from his lips like air from a slow puncture. Tyler staggered to his feet and gave him an apologetic look. "Yeah, I know. That was dirty pool."

Jade sword and cavalry sabre met with a crash like thunder, sending out sparks like startled fireflies. Ryder's jaw hardened as he fought with Yu Lim, thrusting and feinting with his lengthy curved blade while the lithe young girl danced around his attacks, parrying them with her own weapon. She advanced with a downward slash and the outrider felt a sting of pain as the sword traced a cut across his cheek. His head swam and he shook it off. The greenish blade shone; something about it made his stomach churn, as if even the mere presence of it was enough to cause him illness. Ryder attacked again in a flurry of stabs and chops, pushing Yu Lim back step after step.

Tyler saw Yu Lim's duel and hesitated; the girl seemed to be holding her own, at least for the moment. Across the trail, he spied Heller by the barn with something small in his hand; the cowboy's eyes widened as he realized just what it was – a dynamite stick. The outrider was trying to light a match, without much success. Tyler's reaction was instant; he ejected a single spent cartridge from his pistol and inserted a fresh one – his last. With a flourish, he brought up the gun and shouted. "Hey!"

Heller turned, lighting the stick as he did so. "Wha'?"

Tyler fired. The shot scraped Heller's hand and he dropped the explosive. The outrider had a split-second to curse himself before the tiny fuse burnt through, and the charge detonated, blowing him apart. The skittish horses fled the sound and trotted into the safety of the barn.

Fivehawk peered cautiously over the window frame, noting the black scorch mark that had only moments ago been Heller. Grabbing his bow and quiver, he beckoned to Tyler, and the cowboy came running.

Yu Lim's eyes narrowed; she had played with this thug long enough. Spinning the jade sword like a whirlwind, she crossed blades with Ryder edge-to-edge, channelling all her energy into the blow. The steel cavalry sabre shattered with the impact, leaving only the ornate grip and a stubby length of metal remaining.

Ryder rocked back in surprise, then snarled, "Curse you!"

"You are defeated, outrider!" she retorted.

A cruel grin crossed his face. "Not quite." Ryder's

thumb flicked a switch on the sabre's hilt and he pointed the broken blade at Yu Lim. A hidden gun mechanism in the handle tripped and fired, sending a shot-blast into her shoulder.

Tyler spun as he heard the shot, but Fivehawk was a moment quicker. Ryder moved to finish Yu Lim off with a stab, standing over her fallen form; in the next second, the Indian nocked an arrow and released it.

The shaft hit Ryder in the throat, lodging in the skin of his neck. His broken weapon fell from his hands and the outrider stumbled away, clutching at the wound.

Tyler raced to the girl, picking her up in his arms. "Ah, Fivehawk. She's hurt bad." Yu Lim mumbled something incoherent. "We gotta get her to safety."

"The inn," the Indian said, "I left some of my saddlebags there. I can fashion medicine for her from the contents."

The cowboy glanced up the mountain. "So much for getting to Drache."

"We still have time – but we cannot let her die."

Tyler nodded. "No question there. But how are we going to get down into the valley? She'll bleed to death before we can ride there."

Fivehawk jerked a thumb at the barn. "The platform."

"Oh, great. The horses, too?"

"The horses too." He took the girl's limp body from Tyler. "Get her weapon as well."

Tyler stooped to pick up the jade sword and turned it over in his hands. "Well, I'll be damned. Take a look at this pig-sticker." He held out the blade to Fivehawk. "It glows. And there's only one other thing I know that does that."

Fivehawk's breath caught in his throat. "Her sword ... the blade is made from sky rock!"

"Right. And it's pure poison to Drache and his outriders. So how come some Chinese girl has it? More to the point, what's she gonna do with it?"

"The jade sword," Yu Lim said weakly, hovering on the edge of consciousness. "It is born from a legacy that fell from the skies…"

"Hush, now," Tyler said to the girl. "Try not to talk."

"No," Yu Lim husked. "If I fall into sleep, I will never awaken. I must not sleep. Must not sleep…"

Fivehawk nodded. "Very well, then." He nodded to Tyler, and the gunslinger helped him place the young woman on his horse. The Indian paused, thinking for a moment. "I have never met a person from your land of China. I would like to hear about it."

Yu Lim gave a wan smile and fought hard to keep the pain from her eyes. Tyler gently led Fivehawk's horse into the interior barn, where his dappled mare was standing, still spooked from the explosion.

The gunslinger studied the barn; large wooden cogwheels set on timber axles were hidden in the shadows of the roof, and hefty ropes as thick as a man's neck connected them to eye-rings in the floor. Tyler discovered a set of levers extending from the floor and tugged one experimentally. Yu Lim moaned in pain when the whole shack shuddered slightly.

Fivehawk shot him a look. "You seem to have found the controls. Be careful."

Tyler gave a half-hearted shrug. "Hey, have you ever known me not to be careful?" Putting his weight behind it, Tyler pulled the lever and the cogs began to spin. With a groan of ice-rimed timbers, the rear half of the barn floor detached and began to sink. In moments, the trio and their mounts were sinking steadily down the sheer cliff-face of Frost Peak, a wall of dark rock on one side, and a heart-stopping drop on the other. Fivehawk chanced a glance over the side of the makeshift elevator and felt his heart leap into his throat. The ropes overhead creaked and complained like old bones; one break, one snap of threads, and they would fall crashing to jagged death on the hard valley floor.

Tyler seemed to shrink into his coat as the wind tugged at the platform, and he looked away from the edge. "So, tell us all about China, hey?" he said with false brightness, trying to keep their minds off their precarious position.

Yu Lim nodded and began to speak; her pain was all that concerned her, and as they carried the Chinese girl down and down into the valley, Yu Lim spilled out the truth of why she had come to the West.

5: THE JADE SWORD

She told the story in mumbles and breathy whispers, sometimes lapsing into silence for a moment before beginning anew. Through the chilly streets of Winterville, Tyler and Fivehawk stole Yu Lim back to the inn, hiding their horses in the stables and carrying the girl up into their room. The noise of the saloon covered their stealthy return, and the old bartender was too busy with his customers to give a moment's thought to them.

Tyler did as Fivehawk asked him, stripping lengths of bedsheet to create makeshift bandages, fetching water to clean the wound, doing the best he could to help the Indian heal her; for his part, Fivehawk said little, simply worked at mixing solutions from his medicine bundle and the nondescript bunches of twigs in his saddlebags. Yu Lim's pale skin glistened like porcelain in the soft light of the lamp, her eyes out of focus, concentrating on a place very far from here.

She never cried out once; she just told them the tale of the blade.

* * *

In the time of legends there came a day when the sky itself was cut in half by a bright comet; so brilliant it was that the scriptures say all of China stood aside from their labours, from peasants in rice paddies to the emperor himself, just to watch it pass overhead. The people breathed a sigh of relief when the dark omen vanished over the horizon, because they knew the comet had fallen off the edge of the world, and that they were free of it.

But this was not the way of things. Unseen by all but a few men, the comet spat a jade egg into the air over the great mountains, and this stone, as big as a man, fell to the earth, landing in the northern plains. The egg's landing had the force of a typhoon, and it killed a troop of bandits that had come to watch the spectacle; all save one.

Now this bandit, whose name was Black Tze, crawled into the crater made by the egg to find that its shell had split into nine pieces, and inside was a glorious crystal yolk made of sapphire. Tze fashioned the yolk into a necklace and when he wore it, his strength doubled, his head grew, his heart turned even blacker than his name and his very blood ran green instead of red. Tze became the terror of the north, because with the sapphire yolk he was able to commit deeds of unspeakable evil; he inflicted terror and death all around him with a mere touch, and summoned an army of the *kuang shi* – the living dead – to build him a castle on the spot where the egg had fallen.

But to Black Tze and his undead soldiers, the jade eggshell was like a venom, and he had his human slaves bury the pieces in the deepest caverns of the world. And so they did — all but one fragment, the smallest, which a noble monk spirited away in dead of night to the emperor's court.

Knowing that Tze's foul powers would soon grow to challenge even his dominion, the emperor charged the monk with fashioning a blade from the jade eggshell, and he ordered a temple built in the mountains where the monk might meditate on how to defeat the evil sorcerer. In time, the eggshell was carved into a jade sword and the monk himself, whose name was never spoken, took it to Black Tze's castle and fought him with it.

The battle raged for many days and nights until the greedy Tze — still a bandit and thief at heart — was distracted by a gold coin the monk tossed into the air. The monk cut across Tze's neck, shattering the sapphire yolk into powder and cutting off his head. But while the sorcerer's body turned to dust, his head laughed and taunted the monk. Before his evil spirit was taken to the darkest of all the hells, Black Tze told the monk that his necklace was just a seedling, the merest shard of a much greater misery that had come to rest in a land far across the ocean.

As his skull fell into pieces, Tze's mocking laughter promised that, even though it might take hundreds of years, when three stars in the western sky shone as one, a force of evil would be unleashed, so huge that it would eat the world whole.

It was the middle of the night when Fivehawk had finished, and Yu Lim's pallor had diminished. Tyler noted that the Indian had left his own wounds untended until the girl had been cared for. Her shoulder now swaddled in bandages, she sat up carefully and tested her injured arm.

She flinched. "Ah. It is difficult to move. Perhaps if I could strap it…"

Fivehawk hesitated, then tugged a blue bandanna from one of his pockets. "Here. Use this to take the weight."

Yu Lim took the square of cloth and turned it over in her hands. "This … this was given as a gift to you, was it not? I cannot accept."

The Indian nodded, thinking of the child Rafe and his family, whose lives he and Tyler had saved. "It was, from a brave boy I know. He would be pleased to have someone as courageous as you make use of it."

She smiled, and unspoken warmth travelled between them. "Thank you."

Tyler wrinkled his face at the exchange and coughed. "So what happened then?"

"What do you mean?"

"The story about the sword." He indicated the

68

blade, back in its scabbard on the empty bed nearby. "What happened after old Blackie died?"

"Ah." Yu Lim worked the bandanna around her arm. "The legend says that the emperor told the monk to keep the blade at the secret temple, and prepare for the return of Tze's spirit. But the monk knew that the only way to seal Tze in hell was to find the rest of the comet and destroy it, so he passed on his scriptures to his son, and then that son gave them to his son and so on down through the ages, until the time when the white men came with their ships."

Fivehawk shook his head. "If I did not hear this with my own ears, I would think it was a lie. It is the legend of The Faceless, of how a part of it must have touched your land. Your story mirrors my people's tale of the prophecy ... that warriors will face the beast again when the three stars meet."

Yu Lim nodded gravely. "Yes, it seems so. My *sifu* chose me as the bearer of the jade sword, and so I have come here, to do all I can to end the dominion of this darkness."

"Why you, though?" Tyler asked. "I mean, no offence, but why send a girl to do a –" he paused, fumbling for the right word – "a monk's job?"

"Demons are afraid of women," she retorted with a sniff. "Everyone knows this. Besides, I have lived in the temple since my childhood, training to carry the blade. I have no other path than this one. I was chosen."

"Chosen? What, to be some kinda monster-killer, some kinda slayer?"

Yu Lim pulled a face. "Nothing so silly. I have a duty and I swore on the life of my *sifu* that I would fulfil it."

"This see-foo…" Fivehawk struggled with the word. "He is your father?"

"My teacher. He is dead now."

"I am sorry."

For a moment, Yu Lim's tough exterior dropped away and both men caught a glimpse of her soul. "One day a group of brigands found the temple and looted it, searching for the jade sword, but it was not there. *Sifu* had sent me into the mountains with it, to train and hunt. When he would not tell them where I was, they tortured this poor, frail old man for three days before they burnt the temple to the ground and left him to die." She blinked back tears and gave a shaky smile. "Even in death, he had a lesson for me. He taught me that the greatest, hardest duty is to hold evil at bay rather than to defeat it."

"He was a wise man," Fivehawk said carefully.

"Yes," Yu Lim snapped, getting up from the bed. "Now I must honour his memory. We must return to the mountain." Like vapour, her moment of fragility had vanished into the air.

Tyler held up his hands, palms out. "Now whoa there, just a minute, miss! If there is one thing I have learnt the hard way, it's that going after that highbinder Drache without any kinda plan is just plain stupid! Every time we tried that, we've been shot at or strangled or blown up or burnt or near-drowned!"

"You forgot 'buried alive'," added Fivehawk.

"Well, yeah, almost buried alive too! If we're gonna be partners, we need to think before we act!" Tyler paused and his face fell. "Boy, I *never* thought I'd hear myself say that."

Yu Lim frowned. "What do you propose?"

The cowboy chewed his lip. "Well, first we need to find another way up that mountain. We sure can't take the trail or use that rope-elevator thing again."

Fivehawk moved to the window and took a careful look outside. "True, they'll be watching for us." He sighed. "If only we knew what that creature Drache is doing atop the mountain … we could get there only to find a fortified camp and a hundred more of his outriders waiting for us."

"He has built something sinister up there, but I know not what it is," Yu Lim said. "Only that the workers taken up to the summit never return again."

Tyler shuddered as he thought of the crevasse. "Those poor beggars."

A glitter of light from the edge of town caught Fivehawk's eye: the water tower. "What about this iron track Drache has made your people lay?"

"Yeah, the railroad. That leads into the mountains, right?" Tyler asked.

"Yes, to the very top," Yu Lim replied. "But it follows no path I could understand. It crosses itself and circles foothills when a straight line would be far quicker to make."

Tyler shook his head. "Great, that's another question we can add to the pile. Where does Drache's railroad go to?"

"Everything about this demon that walks among men is part of some greater design," Fivehawk gritted. "Everything Drache has done so far has been part of a scheme laid out by The Faceless — kidnapping the people from Stonetree and Black Bear Valley, digging in the Burnt Hills for the sky rock and now these insane constructions in Winterville. We are all of us two steps behind him, too far off the Spirit Road to see clearly. We must learn his ultimate goal!"

"Drache will awaken the beast, the spirit that once controlled Black Tze. That is obvious." Yu Lim frowned.

"But how?" Fivehawk asked. He nodded at the sky. "The time draws nears when the stars will meet. Before that happens, we must know Drache's intent ... where and how he will commit this foul deed."

Tyler blew out a breath and sat heavily. "Look, forgetting all your redskin and Chinese mumbo-jumbo monster stories for a second, I agree with you in principle. Magic swords, twinkling stars and crazy railroads don't mean a damn thing to me, but giving that filthy motherless fourflusher a necktie party is certainly going to do the world a favour." He stifled a yawn. "But now ain't the time."

"What do you mean?" Yu Lim asked hotly.

"Look at us! Fivehawk and me, we're beat up and dead on our feet, and you? Well, miss, you appear to be one arm short."

She grabbed the sword with her good arm and waved it menacingly at Tyler. "I have always said I could fight a man with one arm tied behind my back! I could demonstrate!"

Fivehawk shook his head. "Yu Lim, he's right. We must rest. The healing herbs I poured on your wounds will need a few hours to work, and we could all use some sleep." He pulled the shutters on the window half-closed. "Drache's men are still out looking for us … we'll be safe here for a while."

Yu Lim opened her mouth to protest, then hesitated. "Very well. Until dawn, then?"

Fivehawk settled into a chair, carefully positioning himself with his rifle across his lap, aimed at the locked door. "Until dawn." He glanced across at Tyler; the paleface was already asleep, snoring lightly with his hat over his eyes.

In moments, the three of them had surrendered to fatigue and fallen silent.

The air inside the Black Train was pleasantly warm, despite the sheer cold of the Frost Peak winds that

73

howled around the carriage and the nearby Terminus. Drache made a contented clicking sound with his teeth, and smiled. Arrayed in front of him were dozens of blueprints and papers, a crazy paving of plans and diagrams that threatened to spill over the edges of his ornate desk and on to the floor of his study. He paused to take a sip of brandy and noticed the time on the tall grandfather clock by the door. Drache allowed himself a moment to review his life, and discovered that he could not remember the last time he had ever needed to sleep.

An odd pang of regret touched him, and he waved it away as if it were a nagging insect. As if that were important – sleep was a thing for the weak and the ordinary, and Drache's ability to do without it was just one more of the benefits laid to him by his most glorious benefactor.

Even thinking of the benefactor made Drache turn towards The Instrument, the spherical object carved from some unnatural, unearthly wood settled quietly on its brass stand. Quiet. Quiet and ever watchful. He scowled at it and looked away. *Soon*, he told himself, *soon I will have no more need of that infernal machine*.

He shuffled through the papers until he found the one he wanted; it was a map of the local area, with the county borders marked out in thick, dark lines. Drache traced them with a meaty finger, following the lighter red ink that circled just inside the borderline. How hard had he searched to find a place like this, in all of North America? To find a place where the veins of mineral came together in just the right quantities, where the lines of natural magnetism in the Earth herself intertwined like threads in a rope. A place where a mountain shot high enough to meet his needs. He held in a laugh. No time for that now. He would allow himself laughter when his task was complete – and then it would be the bellicose roar of a god's humour, enough to make the world tremble in its wake. He laid the map carefully atop his desk, and patted it like a well-behaved animal. Drache nodded with admiration at his own creation, the perfect shape he had created.

"And once you are complete, my fabulous, extraordinary design, I will reduce every living thing within these borders to ash and ruins."

Something rattled beyond the study door and Drache felt the room move slightly as someone entered the anteroom. "Master Drache?" called a voice. "Sir?"

Drache replaced his pince-nez glasses and stormed to the door, wrenching it open. Skale, a skeletal outrider, stood before him, arms twitching in front of him like those of a preying mantis. "Never disturb me in my study!" Drache yelled.

"S-sir!" Skale quaked. "Our informant in the town has reported some new arrivals at the inn—"

"You interrupt my work for that old fool's hearsay and gossip?" he snarled.

"Oh, no sir! Outside, sir! You must see this! I thought you would want to—"

Drache pushed the outrider aside and stepped out of the anteroom, down the steps set into the carriage's footwell. He strode from the train and across the cold earth to the Terminus dome, ignoring the snow and the chill that cut bone-deep.

"Here he is, sir." Skale bounded to Drache's side in long-legged steps, and pointed. Ryder stood before them, his coat soaked on one side with verdant blood, and an arrow stuck through his neck.

"What is this?" Drache growled. Ryder tried to speak, but only rattling sounds came forth. Drache shook his head in frustration and with one savage movement, he grabbed the arrow shaft and tore it from the outrider's throat, ripping through skin.

Ryder gave a gargling scream and his hands flailed; Drache grabbed him by the neck and held the torn flesh together. The rail baron paused to study the arrow in his other hand, then snapped it in two. "Talk to me, Ryder."

The outrider's words were thick and fluid. "Indian and a gunslinger. 'Nother one too. Targaah. Wanted them dead. They killt Hellah. Grizzly's gone, don' know where."

"Targa, you insolent witch!" Drache spat. "She swore they were dead! They still live, and yet she has said nothing to me!" His voice dropped. "Did you kill them, Ryder? The Indian and the gunslinger?"

"No," he coughed wetly. "Still 'live."

"Bah!" Drache shouted and pushed Ryder away. The outrider began choking. "Skale!" Drache barked. "Get him out of my sight, and sew him up! I want him alive to share in Targa's punishment!" The rail baron cursed and kicked at the ground. "I'll do more than blind her this time!"

Fivehawk jerked awake from a dreamless sleep with half a word on his lips, and shuddered. The room was quiet, with only the rhythmic breathing of Yu Lim and Tyler in their slumber – that and the occasional drip from the ceiling into the tin bucket by the wall. The Indian rubbed his hands together; they were sweaty. He sighed. There was no enemy at the door, no outrider with a gun in his hand ready to burst in and open fire. He was awake for no reason.

Yu Lim murmured something dreamily in her own tongue and shifted a little on the bed, the knife of moonlight shining through the window catching her profile. Fivehawk had seen many pretty women in his life, from his own tribe and beyond, yet none of them seemed to match the cool exotic lines of the Chinese girl's face. There was something intriguing about her, an inner light that threatened to captivate him should he look at her too long.

Fivehawk made a "Hmph" sound and turned away. These were foolish thoughts to be having at a time like this; it was still deep in the night, and if he were to be even a little rested by sunrise, then he had to sleep. Eyelids drooping, Jonathan's drowsy gaze crossed the window and caught sight of some movement.

He blinked twice and looked again, leaning closer. At the massive iron gates to the strange mansion – the Governess's house, as the bartender had called it – there was a hulking figure tugging at a bell-pull like it was a rope to a drowning man. Even at this distance, Fivehawk recognized the big, hairy outrider they had tangled with only hours before. The bear-like man was shivering uncontrollably, and Fivehawk felt a little sorry for the simple giant. He must have recovered from Tyler's unorthodox attack and stumbled blindly down the mountainside, finally arriving here, in town. There was no sign of the one who shot Yu Lim, however.

The Indian reached down to the shelf under the window. There, where he had left it, was Tyler's spyglass. He opened up the telescope and rubbed condensation from the lenses with his sleeve. What he saw next gave him pause.

Three figures in dark swaddling clothes were advancing from the house, through the gnarled and twisted trunks of the trees that dotted the mansion's arcane garden. They were women, he was sure of it, from their gait and movement. The figure in the centre pulled back an ermine-lined hood to reveal a face, and Fivehawk raised the telescope to his eye. The woman's face came into clear view and he gasped – Targa! There was no mistaking that red-haired harpy ... she seemed different somehow, with what appeared to be a blindfold over her eyes and a strange clasp binding her hair at her neck, but it was unquestionably Targa. The same woman who had sent a pack of mindless townsfolk to murder him – Drache's mercenary. Targa exchanged words with the other two, commands of some sort, and they nodded in perfect unison, moving to walk ahead of her. Fivehawk frowned. Perhaps Targa had her own coterie of bodyguards now ... a likelihood given that it was a good chance that she was the Governess the old coot downstairs had spoken of. As he had done with Stonetree and Burnt Hills, Drache had left Winterville in the charge of one of his favoured minions.

The scene unfolded in silence; they were too far away for him to hear through the closed window, and he dared not open it. Their backs to him, the two other women mirrored Targa's actions and dropped their hoods before opening the gates. The big man was making small, helpless gestures. *Probably apologizing for not murdering us*, Fivehawk thought. Targa's response was as expected; she backhanded the outrider across the face and then cuffed him again as he walked into the garden. The Indian gave a half-smile. *We'll beat you yet*, he told Targa silently. *You and your Master*.

The other women began closing the gates, and the nearest one turned back as she did so. Fivehawk studied the face: a ghost-white complexion with haunted eyes and straw-coloured hair, once more bound back with the same glittering obsidian clasp. She nodded to her counterpart as the other girl stepped into view.

For Fivehawk, it was as if a lightning bolt had flashed out of the cold black sky and struck his heart dead; he felt his pulse miss a beat, his legs turn to water.

The second woman glanced up into the night and let out a breath. Her hair was as black as coal, her skin a tawny shade a brushstroke lighter than Fivehawk's own.

She had eyes the colour of a sunset – she was his sister.

6: EYES-LIKE-AMBER

For a second, Fivehawk felt like he would drown in panic; his mind flew off in a hundred directions at once. Should he open the window and call out to her? Had he made a mistake? Was this a trick set up by Drache to lure him in? He gripped the spyglass tightly in his hands, all fatigue and thoughts of sleep suddenly gone from him. In those moments, his world narrowed down to a tunnel that connected him to his sister as she slowly began to walk back to the Governess's mansion, her face vanishing as she pulled up the hood of her coat. Along with the milk-pale woman, Fivehawk's sister followed Targa and the chastised outrider into the building and closed the huge oaken doors behind them. The Indian jerked with reaction, as if he had been stung.

My sister! he cried out silently. *I search for her for months only to find her in the camp of my greatest enemy? This cannot be!* He looked to the night sky beseechingly. *Great Spirit, is what I see the truth, or some illusion cast by The Faceless?* Fivehawk felt sick dread in his gut. Try as he might to convince himself that it was all some elaborate ruse, he knew the truth as surely as he knew the sun would rise. Somehow, some way, the insidious influence of the demon had touched his sister and bewitched her, magicked her into its dominion by force of will. He could not believe otherwise, that she might willingly ally herself with The Faceless, in the manner that the rail baron Drache had freely committed his whole spirit to the darkness.

"You are Eyes-Like-Amber," he whispered to her, "daughter of Elk's Brother, sister of Fivehawk. Blood of my blood, I swear I will deliver you from this horror."

With purpose, he stood and folded the spyglass – and then paused. Tyler and Yu Lim lay atop the two beds in the room, sound asleep. At once, the floodgates in his mind re-opened and drenched him with conflicts. It would be the most simple of things for Fivehawk to sneak out of the inn and never even wake them, to steal out to the street and find his way to the townhouse; but what would his friends think of him then?

Fivehawk took a step forward and reached out a hand to Tyler's sleeping form; but his fingers stopped inches short of his friend's shoulder. The gunslinger shifted in his sleep, and the Indian tensed, suddenly afraid that he had woken the white man. Instead, Tyler let out a gasp of air, still deep in a sound, dreamless slumber. Fivehawk's hand hovered where he held it as he considered for a moment. He knew that if he woke Tyler and the girl, even though they would promise to help him, they would bicker and talk over what they might do, round and round in circles until the sun came up ... and by then it might be too late. And worse still, he wondered, did he really have the right to risk their lives in a quest that was his and his alone? To come together to fight Drache and The Faceless was one thing; but to rescue Amber was another.

He shook his head with finality; no, this was a personal matter, a question of family, of blood. Fivehawk had not interfered when Tyler had ventured into Drache's mineworks to rescue his kidnapped uncle, and so the paleface should stand aside to let him bring Eyes-Like-Amber back. He had to act now. Fivehawk's hands balled into fists. Every second he stood in this room debating with himself about what to do, Amber was suffering another second under Targa's poisonous influence. The decision was made, then; but he would not leave them without an explanation. Quickly and deftly, Fivehawk removed a small wooden box from one of Tyler's saddlebags and opened it; inside was a fountain pen and a few scraps of paper, and in a shaky, unpractised hand, the Indian wrote a note before placing it on the nightstand.

He gave Tyler and Yu Lim a last look, then gathered his weapons and crossed the room, as silent as smoke. The rifle he left by Yu Lim's side; this would need to be a soundless assault. The well-oiled door did not betray his passing, and in moments he was outside, hidden in the shadows from the moonlight and the windborne snow. Fivehawk took a deep breath and calmed his mind. *I must not falter*, he told himself. *My sister's life depends on it*. He mouthed a prayer to the Great Spirit and the old shaman Sleeping Fox to watch over him and protect Amber, a part of him wondering if this might be his last night in the world of the living. If he were to die, would that mean that the prophecy would go unfulfilled and The Faceless would rise unopposed? The Indian considered his father's words to him, the stories of the legend; that two warriors from different peoples would come together in order to defeat it. He licked his dry lips. The myth could just as easily mean that Tyler and Yu Lim were the two, and perhaps bringing them together and setting them on the Spirit Road had already fulfilled Fivehawk's duty. In his heart of hearts, Fivehawk knew that this was a poor excuse and a vague way to explain his rash actions to himself – *Tyler's headstrong nature has infected me*, he thought – but in the end, it was to protect his friends that he let them sleep. For all the times Tyler had saved his life, the last only a few hours ago, he would not oblige him to do it once again; and as for Yu Lim, something of the girl's manner made him want to protect her from harm.

"I do this alone," he said aloud, and then dashed into the night, never once looking back.

"You are pathetic!" Targa shrieked at the cowering Grizzly. "Two men and some slip of a girl, and you let them beat three of you, and the Guardians as well? Drache's dreaded outriders? A gang of school-boys with slingshots would be more fearsome!"

Grizzly squirmed. "They wuz smart, ma'am. The Chinee girl, she hadda sword, see. She bled Ryder with it real good. It was a mighty scary cutter, too. Glowed, it did."

Targa's tone changed in an instant. "Glowed?" she purred. "How, exactly? Think now, Grizzly. This is important."

The outrider licked dry lips. "Uh, it were like the Northern Lights, green it was. It made me feel poorly just looking at it."

"Could it be possible?" she asked herself. "A sword made of that damned stone?" Targa remembered with painful clarity the properties of the mineral nicknamed "sky rock" … it was one of the side-effects of Drache's patronage, she reflected, that the strange stone was toxic to his minions. "And this girl with the sword, she killed Ryder?"

"Uh, no," Grizzly said in a small voice. "I don't rightly know, see. The gunslinger, he musta hit me with some sneaky blackjack or somethin', 'cause next I know I comes to and Ryder's all gone, just some blood on the snow left there and his sabre, all broke like."

Targa's foul temper returned in a trice. "Ha! You useless lummox! I'd kill you myself if I thought it would be worth the effort!" She paced the room between Duske and Dawne. "If Ryder hasn't frozen or bled to death out in some snowdrift, he'll kite back up that mountain and go crying to Drache…"

"What of that?" asked Dawne.

"He'll spill his guts!" Targa snarled. "Then my darling Robur will come gunning for me." She paused. "I must be ready for him…"

"Governess," Dawne said, interrupting from her place by the window. "We have an uninvited guest."

"Show me," said Targa, and the pale woman looked down into the garden. A lone figure dropped down from the wall and skirted around the ornamental pond, towards the mansion's side entrance. Targa smiled thinly and nodded to Dawne. "Let's show him some hospitality, shall we?"

Fivehawk stepped lightly around the edge of the mansion's small grounds, casting a brief look at the gnarled, twisted trees and other unnatural-looking plants that formed the facing garden. He avoided the oval pond, noting the pads of ice that floated on it, and moved to the building, hugging the walls. The Indian ignored the oaken doors and made his way in through the tradesman's entrance. A sprinkle of sulphurous powder on a twig made short work of the lock; he slid inside, fleet-footed and – so he hoped – invisible.

Inside, the mansion was grim and full of shadows. Fivehawk danced from one pool of blackness to the next, pausing at each door he passed in search of sounds, listening for signs of movement within. Presently, he entered a long hall decorated with oil paintings and spitting gas lamps. At the far end stood a figure in an ermine-trimmed coat. His heart caught in his throat.

"Amber," he said quietly and the figure's head rose. *Could it be her?* he wondered. He closed the distance, but not without one hand close to the handle of his tomahawk.

Abruptly, the woman turned and tugged at the coat; the garment flew away as she shrugged out of it, and beneath the hood was revealed a chalky face with golden hair. Fivehawk drew the axe and narrowed his eyes. Dawne simply acknowledged him with a nod and threw up her hands; from hidden spring-holsters in her sleeves, two long daggers emerged, and she came at him in a rush of razor-sharp steel.

Fivehawk blocked one attack, ducked another, grimacing as one of the knives sliced the tip from one of the feathers that he habitually wore in his hair. The Indian spun and caught Dawne off-guard, the tomahawk blade in perfect position to slice open her cheek. He had no stomach to fight women, minions of Drache or not, and flipped the axehead around to swat her with the flat of the blade.

She reeled and twisted away from him, then broke into a run. With a quick glimpse over her shoulder, Dawne ducked through an open door at the end of the corridor. His face set in a grim mask, Fivehawk hefted the weight of his weapon and followed her.

The room was an opulent study, with overstuffed chairs and couches arranged around a roaring fireplace; in the largest of these, a throne-like construction, sat Targa, a glass of brandy in her hand. She smiled under her blindfold.

"Well, greetings to you, Mister Fivehawk, isn't it? I wonder where your little cowboy friend is? Well, no matter."

The Indian said nothing. Dawne stood to Targa's right, her blades still drawn and ready, and at the furthest side of the room was the hairy outrider, kneading the grip of a large revolver. But Fivehawk's mind only registered these things as peripheral facts — his full attention was reserved for the woman who stood behind Targa's chair.

"Amber," he repeated. "I am here."

If his sister understood him, she gave no sign. A questioning look crossed Targa's face. "Her name is Duske. She serves me ... as will you."

"Never." Fivehawk's anger built like a forest fire inside him.

"Your arrival is perfectly timed. You will be just the gift I need to mollify Master Drache..."

"I will not succumb to Ramah. You cannot poison me."

Targa gave a hollow laugh. "That pitiful drug? Believe me, Indian, our benefactor has a method of control far better than some rare desert herb." She smiled. "Come now, be reasonable. Take a seat, share a glass of brandy with us. You'll find me to be excellent company."

Fivehawk's eyes flicked to the low table, with its crystal decanter of liquor, then back to Targa. "Release my sister."

Targa's eyes widened. "*Sister?*" She shot a hard glance at Amber, who withered a little under it. "Oh, what an unexpected piece of fortune! And here was I thinking this little Indian tramp was just some redskin slave girl for me to command." She sipped her drink. "How very naughty of you, Duske. You have been hiding that from me all this time, haven't you? Keeping that secret locked up in your pretty little head?"

"Release her!" Fivehawk almost shouted. "I will not ask again!"

Targa shook her head playfully. "I think not. This is becoming far more interesting..."

Her words were barely spoken when Fivehawk's foot shot out like a striking cobra. His kick flipped the low table into the air and the decanter flew into the fireplace; the alcohol inside instantly burst into flames and belched fire into the room.

Fivehawk moved like lightning as his enemies reeled. Crossing the room, his bow dropping into his hand and an arrow tensing on the string, he pulled it tight and held it inches from Targa's face.

"You savage!" she cried from where she fell, beating at burns on her clothes. "That cognac was imported all the way from France!"

Dawne shifted a little and Fivehawk gave a slow shake of his head. "Move and I will kill your Governess with a single shot."

Targa's skin crawled as the arrow came closer, her mouth suddenly dry. The shaft was tipped not with a common metal head, but with a carved shard of stone that mimicked creamy jade. That damnable sky rock! She felt the peculiar discomfort the mineral produced already coursing through her, knotting her innards and causing her pain. Even as she feared for her life, part of her was considering this new information, that the Indian possessed this special arrowhead...

Targa gestured at Duske, recovering her composure. "It seems this round is yours, Indian. Very well, take her. I still have another set of eyes." She waved her hand, and Duske shivered; Targa's control was suddenly gone.

She blinked, and for the first time it was Eyes-Like-Amber who looked up at her brother. "Jonathan?" she said in a small voice. "Where is this place?"

Fivehawk's heart leapt, but he smothered the emotion just as quickly. They still had to escape with their lives. He jerked his head at the door. "Run Amber, quickly. You must leave."

Like someone who had just awoken from a deep sleep, Eyes-Like-Amber stumbled past him and Fivehawk stepped after her, keeping his aim firmly on Targa. "I will pay you back for this misery tenfold," he said coldly. "Tell your master that!"

As he ducked out into the hall, Dawne and Grizzly made to move after him, but Targa gestured angrily to them. "Fools, help me up!"

"Governess, the Indian escapes..." began Dawne.

"Oh, don't be so stupid!" Targa barked. "Sister or not, she belongs to me!"

Fivehawk and Amber raced through the mansion's corridors to a wide reception hall that opened on to the main entrance. Feet clicking across a floor of wide flagstones, he pressed at the doors; a bulky deadlock held them closed.

"I cannot force this open..." he murmured, looking around for another exit.

"Brother," Amber said quietly, rubbing at her face, her neck. "You came for me. Thank you." She smiled wanly. "I feel as if I am in a dream."

"This is no dream, sister. We will be trapped here if we cannot open these doors."

Amber brightened suddenly. "I remember! There

is a switch here..." She stepped to the wall, where an elaborate candelabra stood on a pedestal. She pulled on it, and the ornament turned in place.

Fivehawk could not help but smile at his sibling. "A hidden control? How did you know it was there?"

Amber looked back at him. Her expression changed to that of a coy child. "The Governess Targa showed me." She shifted the hidden switch and stone ground on stone beneath Fivehawk's feet.

The Indian had a moment to spare his sister a look of pure hurt at her betrayal before the flagstone on which he stood dropped away and he fell into darkness, bouncing on to a slide and down into the depths of the building.

Targa and Dawne emerged from the corridor and the Governess clapped her hands together. "Duske, come here."

For a long moment, conflicting emotions crossed Amber's tawny face – fear, anger, love, hate.

"Come here!" Targa barked, and at last Duske nodded and obeyed. Targa strode away. "The study, I think. I imagine this one will give us a little more sport than poor Mantooth did."

Fivehawk dropped into Targa's deadly maze and rolled to his feet, the hatchway slamming shut behind him. He blinked in the half-light, his eyes dark with anger. He cursed himself. How could he have been foolish enough to think that Targa would give Amber up so easily? He mulled over her words in the study, thinking back to her dismissal of Ramah as "a pitiful drug". And yet, it had been this very herb that Drache's minions had used to control the minds of an entire town populace. Fivehawk had assumed that this potion was being used to control Eyes-Like-Amber and the other woman as well, but the mistake had been his. Ramah was extremely rare, and it was unlikely much of a crop was left after the use of it at Stonetree. No, Targa had some other hold over these women, some arcane mechanism that Drache had brought her from The Faceless. Fivehawk sighed; hindsight was useless to him now.

It became clear as he weighed it up in his mind. Targa was blinded, so how else could she see but through the eyes of another? Her servants, her "Duske" and "Dawne" were her senses as much as they were her soldiers. And he had been a fool not to see that; his sister was as much a part of Targa as were the Governess's arms and legs. If he could survive to confront her again, he would have to sever that link permanently.

Cautiously, he ventured forward. He was not in a cell, but some kind of corridor, with branching routes and open rooms. The Indian stepped carefully through a doorway and caught a foul stink in his nose. His face wrinkled; the stench of death was in here. He glanced around; the floor was canted at an odd angle, and he saw the faintest tracing of sooty marks in the far corner. He shifted slightly and something clicked below him. Without warning the wall began to close in on him, and the Indian lost his balance for a second, startled by the movement – but only for a second. Summoning up all his strength, Fivehawk threw himself across the rapidly shrinking room towards the closing door on the opposite side, rolling into a ball as he landed. His shoulder caught on the pressing wall, and with a violent tug, he yanked himself free and through, just as the stones sealed the room.

In the study, Targa made a face at the map as the silver ball dropped into the next room. Unseen, Amber touched her face, finding wetness on her cheeks. In a mechanical, disconnected manner she blinked and wiped them dry.

Fivehawk pulled himself to his feet, panting. This next room was as bare as the previous one, except for the floor. Spaced out at a hand-span's distance to each other were holes maybe two inches across. The Indian rubbed his chin in thought. A drain, perhaps, or maybe a place to let something in? With cold certainty he knew that the only way he would know would be to cross the room. As each door opened ahead of him, the one behind closed, meaning the only way out – if there *was* a way – was through.

Taking a deep breath, Fivehawk carefully tried to pick his way around the holes; but the design of the room was too clever for that, for each was just too close to the others to be avoided. When he was a third of the way across, Fivehawk felt a rush of air from one of the holes; he twisted away from it just as a sharpened rod shot up and impaled the roof. Then another emerged, and another. The trap room became a forest of razor-sharp spikes, each one cutting closer to him as he found himself rapidly running out of space. The Indian shouted a wordless cry of defiance and jumped the last few feet to the open exit – as he crossed the threshold, a last spike slashed through his trousers and cut a broad gash up his leg.

Targa's raucous laughter died in her throat when the study window clattered open. She froze as a massive black crow pecked at the latch and then swept into the room, bringing cold air and the light of the approaching dawn with it.

Grizzly sneered at the bird and drew his gun. "Justa dumb stupid crow!"

"Put up that pistol, you ignorant oaf!" said the animal, and the outrider's face went pale with shock. Targa tried not to react to the voice; those were Drache's words, broadcast from a brass medallion that hung around the crow's neck. Another of his machines, it worked like a telegraph for pictures and sounds. The crow cawed and shook, presenting itself to Targa as it settled on a chair back.

"You once again try, and fail, to deceive me, Targa." Drache's words were hot with anger. "Bring your two wenches and come to the Terminus at once! I would have words with you about your deeds!"

"Master Drache," she began, in a falsely calm tone, "I have at this moment the Indian in my possession—"

"Silence!" he roared, and the crow fluttered its wings. "Come to me now or I will strike you dead where you stand!" The bird squawked and took off, back out into the air.

Targa stood and made a show of composing herself.

"But the intruder—" said Dawne. Targa silenced her with a raised hand.

"If I disobey him, he'll murder us in a fit of rage. In person, perhaps I can change his mind." Targa pressed a hand to her head, rubbing away an ache. "The Indian will be dead soon." She glanced at Amber. "If he's not dead already."

The wound burnt like a brand, and Fivehawk snapped off a length of twine from his belt to bind it, tying up the slash. This room was all stone – floor, walls and ceiling – cold and damp with the winter air.

"I must be close to the ground outside," he said aloud. He pulled his tomahawk and tapped it lightly on the rocky walls, listening for an indication that one might have a hollow space behind it. He forced the thin edge of the blade into the gap between two of the stones and put his weight to it, but to no effect.

A drip of water fell from the ceiling on to his face, and he wiped it away. Fivehawk looked up to search for the source as the drip became a trickle, then a stream, and suddenly a flood. In moments, the icy water had reached his ankles. The Indian saw a faint chink of light above him – the freezing liquid was rushing in from the garden's ornamental pond above, and it would fill the tiny room in moments.

7: COLD FIRE

Tyler awoke with a sneeze violent enough to take his hat off his face. He yawned widely, blinked and rubbed the sleep from his eyes, peering around the room. Watery sunlight struggled through the window, and beyond, the snow that had started falling last night was now coming down in clumps.

He stretched and his bones complained; funny how he always seemed to sleep too much on a real bed. He registered Yu Lim atop Fivehawk's bed, her chest rising and falling with each breath, and the Indian's Springfield rifle beside her. Tyler blinked at the chair where Fivehawk had been sitting, and did a double take.

"Holy Cats!" he blurted, stumbling to his feet. "Where the heck is he?" Tyler's eyes darted left and right; none of their gear was missing, except for some of Fivehawk's kit – his bow and quiver, to be exact. "Ah, no..." The first inkling that his trail buddy had done something very foolish came to Tyler as he noticed the folded square of paper on the nightstand. He grabbed it and began to read.

"Ah, for Pete's sake!" he cried. "You dumb, loco featherhead!"

Yu Lim stirred and stretched like a cat. "Is it dawn already?" she slurred, favouring her injured arm. "Where's Fivehawk?"

Tyler grabbed his coat and tugged it on. "I'll tell you where," he grated. "He's on his way to the bone orchard if we don't stop him!" He tossed the paper to her. "Man alive, that stubborn redskin never listens to me!"

Yu Lim glanced at the note. "I can't read your language. What does it say?"

"His sister – claims he saw her in yonder mansion. He must've lit out while we were asleep."

The Chinese girl went to the window. "Would he do such a thing?"

"Normally, my answer would be no, but since we got here Fivehawk ain't been his usual self." Tyler spun the chamber on his Peacemaker experimentally and flipped it into his holster. "He can't think straight for his sister being gone."

"He would risk his life for her? Risk everything?"

Tyler paused and looked at her squarely. "Wouldn't you?"

She nodded. "How long has he been gone?"

"Ink's still fresh; an hour, maybe two."

"Then we should—" Yu Lim halted in mid-sentence, her attention caught by something outside.

"What is it?" Tyler asked, peering over her shoulder.

"Look there! Red-hair is leaving the mansion." Sure enough, Targa and her two bodyguards were riding out of the gates at a fast clip, with a fat crow swooping and diving around them.

Tyler's balled fist smacked into the windowsill. "Targa. So she's this 'Governess' that old coot mentioned!"

Yu Lim nodded. "You did not know?"

Tyler shook his head, watching as the trio vanished into the thickening snowfall, heading out of town.

"They did not have him with them." Yu Lim's voice held a note of fragile hope. "He could still be alive, as a prisoner."

Tyler's face was grim. To consider the alternative was troubling. "Let's go."

Fivehawk felt the energy fading from his arms and legs like melting snow in the sunlight. The icy waters from the pond were gushing in ever faster, now up past his waist and still climbing. His buckskin clothes were heavy with the foetid fluid, and his feet struggled to keep him upright on the slick stones beneath them. Twice he came off-balance and his head went under, filling with brackish liquid that seared his bare skin with its chill. With effort he slammed the tomahawk into the door that had shut him into this room, but it was fashioned from sturdy, varnished ironwood that made it just as impenetrable as the stone surrounding it. The cold invaded him, wrapping every inch of his body in a frosty embrace. Fleeting images of the dead men he had seen in the crevasse returned to him; soon he would join them, frozen like a statue in the infinite, never-ending cold. Even his thoughts were slowing, as if the frigid waters were weighing them down as well. He would never see Amber again, never know if she would be free of Targa's control. He tried to comfort himself with thoughts of Tyler and Yu Lim; he trusted them. Fivehawk knew in his heart that they would not fail. They could not.

The tomahawk fell from his numb fingers and disappeared into the water; the Indian could no longer feel his hands and feet, just the chill as it sucked him dry.

Above, the sky winked through the falling water, taunting him.

The mansion's gates were massive constructions of ironwork, secured with a lock made of boilerplate. Tyler spat into the snow. "Ah, heck. I left my dynamite with the horses."

Yu Lim gave a curt smile. "One tree does not make a forest." In a single fluid movement, she drew the jade sword from its scabbard on her back and brought it down on the tongue of the lock, her breath hissing out from between her teeth. The blade bit into the iron and split it in a shower of sparks.

"Wow. You're really handy with that thing," said Tyler, shifting open the gate.

"And now?" Yu Lim asked.

Tyler drew his gun and cocked the hammer. "Now we wake up the neighbours."

Something in Fivehawk's mind flared like a lit match; *No!* it cried, *You will not die here today! Fight, son of Elk's Brother, fight for life!*

The Indian spat out water as it splashed over his face and threatened to engulf him. In moments, he would go under for the last time and never rise.

Fight! said the voice. *Die today and the world will be doomed with you!*

The icy liquid swamped Fivehawk's head, and the cold was like a blow across the face. He saw a hazy shape, a kindly old face with skin like sun-dried leather, a hand reaching out to him. *Know the eagle,* the old man said, *take his strength and fly free!* At the edge of consciousness, Fivehawk felt the aged shaman beckoning him, encouraging him.

He coiled the last of his reserves into himself and pushed at the stone floor, breaking the surface of the water like a leaping salmon, hands outstretched towards daylight. For an impossible second, Fivehawk seemed to hang there; then his fingers found purchase and held.

But the effort had been too great. Drained, the

Indian dangled over the filling stone cell, too weak to pull himself up, just feet from safety.

They burst into the garden like shots from a cannon, rushing through the bare flowerbeds and gnarled trees towards the mansion. Tyler cried out as he caught sight of movement on the rooftop and tackled Yu Lim to the frozen earth. A massive .50-90-calibre bullet blew a fist-sized chunk from a tree trunk above them.

A metallic click-click sounded through the chilly air. "He's reloading," Tyler said. "Gotta have himself a buffalo gun, a Sharps maybe."

"A rifle?" Yu Lim asked.

"More like an artillery piece. One hit from that'll turn a man into dog food."

As if to illustrate the point, the gun barked and a branch overhead shattered into wood shavings. Tyler retorted with two blasts from his Peacemaker, which whined off the stone parapet. Crouched behind it, Grizzly worked the action and loaded another bullet into the chamber.

"You cannot hit him while he hides behind the ledge," Yu Lim hissed. "You need to draw his fire."

Tyler chewed his lip. "Yeah, but I can't run and take aim at the same—" He never finished his sentence; with a wiggle of her hips, the Chinese girl was suddenly up and running, dashing across the open towards the ornamental pond.

"You crazy little calico! Keep your head down!" he cried, glancing up as he saw Grizzly's shadow move.

The outrider squinted through the Sharps' raised peep sight and took aim at the running figure's back. "Sword won't stop no lead, missy..." he husked.

Tyler thumbed back his six-gun's hammer and raised his arm; he took half a breath to aim and then tightened his finger on the trigger. The shot struck Grizzly through the gun sight and he pitched forward over the parapet. The outrider fell silently to the ground and lay there, still.

Yu Lim was beckoning him frantically as Tyler ran to her side. "I swear, I don't know who's the more haywire, Fivehawk for running off or you for pulling such a darn fool antic as that!"

The woman ignored him and flipped over into the pond, which seemed now to hold only a few inches of water. Tyler could have sworn that it was full to the brim when he'd seen it from the hotel window.

"Down here, look!" She pointed. The water was rushing though a grille set in the floor of the pond. "Help me get this up! Someone is trapped in there!"

Tyler followed her over, and added his muscles to Yu Lim's. With a joint cry of effort, they pulled the iron grid open. Through the cascading water, a hollow face plastered with wet streaks of black hair was visible.

"Fivehawk!" Tyler cried, and dropped to his knees, extending his hands into the darkness of the stone cell. "Take my hand, man!"

The Indian's gaze seemed to be focussed elsewhere, as if he were unaware of Tyler's presence. Without a sound from him, Fivehawk's grip began to falter.

"Fivehawk!" Tyler shouted again. "Wake up, Redskin! Fight it!"

The last words did the trick, and the light snapped on in his eyes. Their fingers met, grabbed hold, and with a tug, Tyler dragged the Indian out into the daylight.

For a moment, the three of them sat in the draining pond, all shivering in the falling snow.

"Thank you," Fivehawk managed.

Tyler made a face. "I oughta push you back down there. What kind of partner are you, leaving his compadres without a word? Ain't we all learnt by now, teamwork is what goes?"

"I h-had no ch-choice," Fivehawk chattered. "You would have done the s-same."

Tyler opened his mouth to speak, but Yu Lim put her hand on his arm to stop him. "Yes, we would have. But there are no lone warriors here. From now on, we fight as one."

"F-forgive me."

Tyler rolled his eyes. "Ah, it ain't nothing." He stood. "Come on, let's get outta here and get some fresh duds. Targa's riding for the mountain and there's no time like the present."

"My suh-sister is with her."

Yu Lim glanced up to study the storm clouds advancing on the valley. "Then we will rescue her."

Their fastest horses were spent by the time they reached the Terminus at the summit of Frost Peak, and the animals panted and wheezed in the cold, with curls of steam showing their hot sweat; but to ride any slower would have been to court Drache's rage even more.

Targa entered the dome with her guards at her side, Dawne's pale face twitchy and watchful, and Amber's half-distracted by distant thoughts. Skale stood nearby, working on Ryder's ruined neck with a needle and thread. The injured outrider looked up, his face drawn and hollow.

"Master, I am here," Targa announced. Drache was where she had left him, standing alone on the green star of tiles, his back to them all. An indistinct object sat at his feet, hidden under purple silk.

Drache turned slowly to face her. "Do you remember where I found you, my dear?" His voice was deceptively light. "In a Comanche prize wagon, ready to be sold as a slave? Has that slipped from your memory in recent years?"

"No," she husked. "You were my saviour."

"Yes, I was." He took a step towards her, and she

tried not to flinch. "And all I asked for in return was loyalty. All I've ever asked from my minions is that." Drache gestured to Skale. "And yet I never seem to get that one, simple thing."

"Master," Targa blurted, "if you would just allow me to explain—"

"For all your intelligence, Targa, you are a contemptuous and shallow woman," he grated. "I allowed you your one and only mistake with Trebuchet, your one sip at the cup of betrayal, but now I see I was too lenient."

A sudden, unbidden flare of defiance sparked in her, as she remembered the Frenchman's strange transformation in the depths of the Burnt Hills mine. "I paid for my error with my eyes! You struck me blind!"

"I did indeed." Drache took her by the arm, his hand like a steel clamp. "In truth I thought you might be tempered by the experience, but it seems to have done little to educate you." He dragged her across the slick tiled floor to the metal wells.

Targa struggled. "No! Please, Master Drache! If only you would listen to me for—"

"No time for last words, Targa. I'm sure one of your handmaidens can do the job of Governess just as well."

"I know where the Indian is!" she shouted in desperation, her foot hovering over the metal pit. The dark steel hummed with invisible power.

Drache hoisted her up and held her in the air. "Do tell." His words were calm, quiet, as if they were discussing the news of the day at a garden party.

"Fivehawk and the gunslinger, the one named Tyler —" her words tumbled out in a rush — "they're in Winterville!"

His face soured. "Oh, I know that already! You'll have to do better!"

"My slave, Duske! She is the Indian's sister!" Her heel glanced off the metal and a spark of static electricity flashed to it, frying a patch of expensive leather. "And there's another, a Chinese girl, with a weapon that could even kill you!"

Drache's face went purple with rage and he tossed her to the tiled floor. "Impudent witch! Explain yourself!"

Targa's heart was hammering in her chest as she sat up; at least he wasn't trying to kill her any more. "She has a sword, a blade made of that lethal stone."

"Impossible! The mine collapsed in on itself, all the sky rock was atomized."

"Perhaps," she managed, trying to recover her dignity, "but she has it nonetheless." Targa glanced at Ryder. "Ask him."

Drache shot a hard glance at the outrider, who nodded. "S'true," he slurred.

"And she isn't the only one. The Indian? He has arrows tipped with it." Targa pulled open the collar of her blouse to show a burn on the side of her neck. "He placed one to my throat."

Drache's eyes clouded in thought. "If the Indian has an arrowhead, then that other young fool may hold a little too." He gave Targa a nod. "This is information I did not have before. Congratulations, my dear. You have just saved your own life." He smiled. "At least for now." Drache glanced at Duske. "Ah yes, I think I see a little family resemblance. Perfect ... she will be just the leverage I need to make those fools bow to me!"

Targa climbed to her feet, and dusted herself down. "I will return to the town and bring them to you." She gestured to her bodyguards, but a bark of laughter from Drache cut her off.

"Oh, no no no. I think you've proven to me more than adequately that I cannot trust you when you're out of my sight." He pointed at the ground. "You and your harpies will stay here, while Skale and Ryder search for them."

Ryder gave a shaky salute and Skale's head bobbed in agreement. "Sir," said the skinny outrider, "do you want them killed, or just broken some?"

"Alive, Skale, alive. Take two men and go down to Winterville. The locals are too afraid to hide them from us, so you should have no trouble finding them. Bring them to me, and their weapons too."

"Need 'orses," Ryder husked through his broken throat.

Drache shook his head. "The train will take you."

Skale and Ryder exchanged nervous glances. The huge, sinister Black Train was a monstrous construct of ebony iron, a bullet-shaped locomotive with a necklace of spikes across its prow which even at rest seemed to be powerful and threatening. None of the outriders liked to ride it, and rumours had spread among them that the engine had no driver or stoker, but was alive itself.

"I will remain here at the Terminus to complete my final preparations. Go now." Drache dismissed them with a wave of his hand.

"Saints 'a' mercy, you're still alive!" The old bartender nearly fell off his chair when the three of them walked in through the inn's entrance. "I-I-I didn't mean to get you all in trouble, now! You gotta understand, I hadda tell them I saw you!"

Tyler tapped Fivehawk on the shoulder. "Go on upstairs and get yourself outta them clothes before you catch a chill. Yu Lim and me will deal with this snarly galoot." The Indian nodded through a shiver and walked away.

The bartender left the table where he'd been sitting and sidled towards the bar, reaching for a shotgun he kept back there. Yu Lim nudged Tyler to call his attention and the cowboy drew his pistol. "Uh-uh, old man. You just keep your hands right where I can see them."

The barkeep smiled a fake, crack-toothed smile. "Hey, looky here. How wuz I to know you'd … er … that is…"

"Not get killed?" said Yu Lim lightly.

Tyler gave a crooked smirk. "So our kind hotelier here took it upon himself to flap his mouth about Fivehawk and me coming into town, right?"

"Everyone in town knows that you don't keep quiet about strangers," the bartender sputtered. "New faces have to be reported! It's a local law, you see, just like paying the—"

"The railroad tax," Tyler interrupted, "Yeah, I remember."

The barkeep took a step back. "Now, you young 'uns gotta know, I had no choice…"

"Really?" Yu Lim's voice held an edge. "You reported any of my people who tried to escape from the work camps, for a reward. I am sure you got the same for turning these two men in."

"Aw, c'mon!" The old man put on a pathetic face. "You wouldn't shoot a kindly old fella, now would ya?"

Keeping his gun steady, Tyler sat at the table, where a half-eaten breakfast of fried eggs and grits was starting to cool. "A kindly old fella, you say?" the gunslinger asked. "No, I guess I wouldn't. But then, you ain't a kindly old fella, are you?" He flashed Yu Lim a wink. "I'll tell you what. You got a laundry out the back, I noticed. My lady friend here is going to help herself to some fresh, dry clothes for my Indian partner, by way of an apology from you."

Yu Lim grinned and took off to find the clean garments. Tyler picked up a forkful of the barkeep's breakfast and began to eat it.

"That's my food!" the old man piped.

"Not any more," Tyler said around a mouthful. "Mmm. Good grits."

"But what'll I tell the folks when they want their duds back?"

Tyler finished off the meal and got up. "You can tell them you had to pay the Tyler tax. Oh, and seeing as how your service has not been of the highest standard, I won't be paying my bill, understand?" He waved the gun at him.

"On the house to you, sir!"

"That's what I thought you'd say."

Fivehawk gave a start when Yu Lim entered the room. "I am not dressed..." he began lamely.

Yu Lim shrugged. "I grew up with six brothers. I lived in a temple full of monks. I have seen many men and their naked—"

"Thank you!" he interrupted, grabbing the bundle of clothes from her. She made a face and turned her back on him, for modesty's sake. He quickly found garments to fit him.

"Your sister..." Yu Lim ventured, keeping watch out of the window. "Is she ... with Drache now?"

112

"No." He almost choked the word out. "I will not consider it. The blind woman, Targa, controls her. If I break that tie, I can save her."

"Fivehawk, you told me that you have come to this desolate place to stop the one called Drache. But will you be able to pass your sister by in order to do it?"

"I can do both!" he grated. "With your help, and Tyler's, I can do it."

She shook her head gently. "You do not believe your own words. I hear it in your voice. You are afraid that she may die, and that you will fail to stop Drache." She turned to face him. "You are afraid you may have to chose between them."

Inner pain glittered in the Indian's eyes. "You are much like her, Yu Lim. Both too wise for one so young. You are correct; I do fear for her." He sighed. "For all of us."

To his surprise, Yu Lim's face broke in a defiant smile. "Even a shrimp may attack a dragon in shallow water. Trust in Heaven, Jonathan Fivehawk. We will shatter Drache's dark designs yet."

He met her gaze, and for a moment, he felt hope return to him.

Tyler pushed open the door. "You decent in here, Fivehawk?" The Indian scowled and buttoned up his new shirt. Tyler made a show of studying him. "Hey, that's real nice on you. You'll want to wear this too, though." He handed over a heavy trail coat.

"That bad weather you said was coming? Well, it's just hit. Take a look-see."

Yu Lim glanced out of the window; the thickening snowfall was now a full-fledged blizzard. "So," she began, "Red-hair abandoned her mansion here in town, so whatever Drache's plans are, it is unlikely we will find evidence of them there."

Fivehawk agreed. "I saw nothing of the sort while I was inside."

"He's a sneaky hombre," Tyler added, "and you can bet he'd never keep anything important where his outlaws could come across it."

"Somewhere safe." The Indian picked up the thread of the conversation. "His kind only trust themselves. He must have a place that is his, and his alone."

A sound cut through the morning air, muffled by the wind and snow but still unnerving and eerie; it was a thin shriek, like the cry of some strange animal, and it echoed around the valley.

"The train's whistle." Yu Lim pressed her face to the window. "The Black Train is here."

Tyler looked Fivehawk squarely in the eye. "I think we just got our answer."

8: THE BLACK TRAIN

Winterville's station was little more than a wooden platform, with a makeshift barn and the tall stick-figure shape of the water tower nearby. Like everything else in the grey, sullen town, it was covered with a thick patina of dirty snow, like the dull monochrome of a tintype photograph. Ryder stepped down from the carriage and walked to where Skale was leading a pair of bony horses out of the stable car.

"What do you reckon?" Skale asked. "We just ride down the street and shoot up the place until they're given up to us?"

Ryder shrugged. "I hate this godforsaken place," he rasped. The stitches in his neck were still fresh and they ached. "Burn it down if you want. Just see that we get Drache his quarry."

Unknown to either of them, Drache's quarries were only a few steps away, peering out from a gap between the doors of a livery stable. Tyler nudged Fivehawk with his elbow. "Looks like that cavalry yahoo is still alive and kicking. He's a little the worse for wear, though."

"The other one, the skinny man. I have not seen him before."

"Yeah. Where does Drache keep getting these trail rats from?"

"There is no shortage of unwise and violent men in the world, Tyler."

The gunslinger sighed. "Ain't that the truth."

"How are we going to get aboard the train?" asked Yu Lim. "We cannot be sure that there are no other outriders."

"That's a chance we'll have to take. Hey, get ready now," Tyler replied. "They're moving."

Skale closed up the stable car and followed Ryder up into the saddle. "That greedy coot at the inn said they took a room at his place ... we should start there."

Ryder nodded. The town was starting to wake up with the morning light, even if no one was braving the snowstorm just yet. "Let's move."

The three of them inched out of the barn and crossed to the railway, dodging between boxes and barrels. A little shorter than a regular train, Drache's loco-motive had several cars strung behind it, with a caboose and a flatbed closest to them.

"We should work our way towards the front," Yu

Lim whispered. "The carriages there are very ornate, probably for Drache's own use."

They ducked past an empty cattle car and Tyler gave an involuntary shiver, as if the wagon was able to render the air around it even colder than it already was. He remembered this rig very clearly; it was one of many that Drache's minions had packed the rail baron's abductees into, for transport to work camps ... or worse.

"Here!" hissed Fivehawk at the next carriage. "The door is not locked." It was a freight wagon, and Tyler peered inside as the Indian boosted Yu Lim up and on board. Wooden boxes, packing crates and tea chests were lashed to the walls inside, some with writing and symbols on them that looked like no language he had ever seen. Fivehawk jumped up next and held a hand out to Tyler. "Quickly!" The gunslinger straightened his hat and climbed in.

Yu Lim took a careful step. "This place. It is not *right*."

"The train?" Tyler asked, looking around. "What do you mean?"

"She is correct." Fivehawk gave a solemn nod. "It knows we are here, like a spider senses vibrations in its web."

"Ah, don't get all spooky on me!" Tyler growled. "A train is a piece of machinery. It's not alive. It's just a big piece of pig-iron on wheels!" He slapped his hand on the wall to illustrate his point. "See? Not alive!"

117

At that moment, the Black Train's ear-splitting whistle screamed through the air like a banshee wail, and a spasm rippled down the length of the carriages. With a crunch of metal on metal, the train began to inch forward on the rails.

Yu Lim and Fivehawk favoured the white man with hard stares and he blinked back at them. "Uh," he managed. "Right?"

Fivehawk yanked at the hatch and pulled it shut.

Ryder whipped his horse around on the spot and glared at the train, in time to catch a sight of the Indian's face disappearing behind the closing door. "What the...?"

"Where is it going?" Skale floundered. "Why would it leave without us?"

Ryder spurred his mount back towards the railroad. "Don't just stand there, slack-jaw! Follow me!"

With a rumble of wheels over points, the train shifted gently, swaying as it moved on to the loop line that would take it back towards the Terminus atop Frost Peak. With another blast from its whistle, the locomotive began to pick up speed, quickly accelerating from the pace of a walking man to that of a cantering horse.

Inside the freight wagon, Fivehawk turned to Yu Lim. "Do you know how to stop this machine?"

The Chinese girl shook her head. "They only expected us to build the rails, not drive the trains on them."

"I reckon I might," Tyler broke in. "I knew a man once, used to be a stoker. He told me all about steam engines when I was a boy."

"Well, you started it. You might as well try to stop it." Yu Lim said.

"Hey, that was just a coincidence."

Fivehawk raised an eyebrow. "Given our past experiences, are you sure?"

Ryder left his horse behind and leapt from the saddle to the gantry on the rear of the caboose. He waved to Skale. "Come on! Jump, you bag of bones!"

With a grimace, Skale did just that and landed hard. "Didn't we just get off this rig?" he complained.

The cavalryman gave him a look of contempt. "I saw that redskin up yonder, reckon those cronies snuck themselves aboard while our backs were turned," his gravelly voice hissed.

Skale's skull-like head bobbed. "This train ain't like no Union Pacific… It starts moving by itself!"

"Quit your whining!" Ryder snapped. "I'm gonna check these carriages one by one, every square inch, until I find those wretched little jaspers. We got eight cars between us and the engine, and they ain't got no place else to go!"

"What about me?" Skale asked.

"Oh, I got a job for you." Ryder pointed at the roof. "Get up there and make your way down to the engine."

"What?"

"Do it! Or else I'll pitch you off myself!"

Skale's face screwed up in worry as he glanced at the landscape passing by; the train's speed was still increasing.

"How fast can this machine go?" Fivehawk asked as they opened the door to the next carriage. "We've left the town behind!"

Tyler set his face in a grim mask. "Well, this being one of Drache's nasty contraptions, there's no telling what it might be capable of."

"Gabriel, are you sure this is safe?" Yu Lim asked as the gunslinger grabbed on to the ladder that would take him up to the wagon's roof.

"Safe? I should say not! But this is the quickest way for me to get to the engine. Once I'm there, I'll hit the brakes and we'll coast to a nice, gentle stop." He swallowed hard. "So I hope."

Fivehawk patted him on the shoulder. "Good luck, Tyler. We'll move up through the carriages and look for any sign of Drache's plans."

"OK!" he yelled, his voice barely carrying over the rush of the wind. "Say, if you come across a ticket inspector, be sure to buy me a return, y'hear?"

Tyler vaulted on to the ice-rimed roof of the wagon and was gone from sight.

The Black Train's steel wheels were a blur of spokes, the pistons along their length pumping more and more speed to the rails as the track straightened out. The railroad that left Winterville bent outward in a gentle arc and then slowly back around the edge of the foothills; these long lengths described part of the county border, but within them, a complex circuit of track sketched an unseen shape across the landscape, criss-crossing itself like a gigantic metal puzzle. The engine's smoky exhaust came in clumps of leaden cloud, streaming from the stubby funnel like the breaths of a charging animal.

Fivehawk and Yu Lim moved quickly down the length of the stable car. The wagon rocked gently from side to side with the motion of the train, the doors to each pen shifting slightly where they had not been secured. The Chinese girl slipped, and the Indian's hand shot out to steady her.

"Ice and straw." She indicated the decking. "I might have fallen…"

Fivehawk waved her into silence. "Our weapons will be no good to us in these close quarters. We must be wary of any adversaries still aboard."

Yu Lim tugged at the door that led to the next car. "You believe there may be others still on the train?"

He frowned. "Drache never leaves this vehicle unguarded."

She replied with a nod and stepped lightly across the open gap between the wagons. Fivehawk followed her and grimaced.

The next wagon was a passenger carriage. Empty bunks topped with rumpled blankets were arranged along one wall, with cupboards and crates in the gaps between them. At the far end, a small part of the wagon was boxed off – a primitive washroom. Yu Lim moved to a round table in the middle of the room and examined it.

"Two chairs," she noted. Laid out in front of them were a scattering of playing cards, poker chips and enamelled mugs of coffee. Yu Lim dipped her finger in the brown liquid. "Still warm."

She looked up to meet Fivehawk's gaze and her face went rigid. The Indian's brow furrowed. "Is something wrong?" he began, the words dying in his mouth as he realized she was staring fixedly at a point over his shoulder. He turned on his heel – too late.

From the shadows in the lee of the doorway, a greasy-looking outrider stepped forward, a Navy Colt pistol in his hand. He spat a gobbet of chewing tobacco to the floor and gave a lopsided grin. "Y'all will find this here carriage is taken." He showed his stained teeth. "Hey! Get out here!"

At his call, the washroom door opened and a

stubby outlaw in a bearskin coat emerged. In one gloved fist he held the bright steel of a large knife. "Huh. You got them good. Like you said."

Bear-coat reached out a hand and touched Yu Lim's hair. "Huh. She's real pretty."

The gunman pulled back the hammer on his weapon. "Well then, maybe we'll keep her. After we deal with her redskin boyfriend here, that is."

Tyler hunched forward as the train rocked, his feet spread to maintain a grip on the boxcar's roof. He inched forward against the rushing air, mumbling a string of cuss-words between each breath. There were a lot of them and he was going through them all, directing the majority at himself and his idiocy for volunteering to take this route. He was just two cars from the engine now, and after a few scary moments where his boots had slipped on patches of thick frost, Tyler was getting into the rhythm of it. The secret was to walk with the movement of the train's rocking motion, not against it, to describe a zigzag path up the carriage instead of a straight one. The Black Train's speed sent the chill wind whipping around him, the cold biting at the exposed skin of his face and tearing the breath from his mouth.

"Almost there, stupid," he said aloud.

The fierce blizzard bore the words back down the length of the train, to where Skale crouched.

Following Tyler's progress, he carefully drew his revolver and took aim at the gunslinger's back.

Fivehawk tensed, ready for an attack, but to his surprise Yu Lim cocked her head under Bear-coat's hand and simpered, batting her eyelashes at him coyly.

"Huh!" the knifeman grunted. "Chinee girly likes me!"

The other outrider made a mock-sad face. "Aww, poor redskin! Them women is always too fickle, ain't they?"

Yu Lim's manner was demure and bashful, and she let out a shrill, childish giggle, tugging her bun of hair to let it fall into a single ponytail. The gunman spat another blob of tobacco out of the corner of his mouth, and for a split-second his eyes flicked away from the Indian. It was all the opportunity Fivehawk needed.

He struck out like lightning, one hand pushing the pistol away towards the window, another hitting the gunman's chest with the heel of his hand; Fivehawk had seen Yu Lim perform a similar move earlier, and to his surprise the attack came easily to him. The Chinese girl's false smile vanished and she flicked her head up and around; the arm's-length of her hair spun up and swatted the knife-wielding outrider squarely in the face.

Fivehawk struggled with the gunman, smashing

his pistol hand into the window frame once, twice, three times. The glass pane gave with a crash and the Navy Colt went spiralling out into the snow.

"I killed ten men to get that cutter!" the outrider roared, his foetid breath filling Fivehawk's nostrils. "You dirty rotten crowbait!" He struck back with a punch that staggered the Indian. "I'll tear ya limb from limb!" With a guttural cry, he shoved Fivehawk towards the carriage's door.

For all his frequent denials to Fivehawk about the ideas of mystic powers and strange forces at work in the world, Tyler nevertheless believed in hunches. His gut instinct had got him out of at least as much trouble as it had got him into; so when a tickle of tension spiked in the back of his neck, something made the gunslinger flash a glance over his shoulder. He saw Skale behind him instantly, a dark shape visible through the snow, the flicker of a silver gun in his hand.

Where the Black Train's wheels met the track, there was a scrape of steel on steel as they clattered over a set of points; the motion vibrated up through the boxcars like an earth tremor.

Fivehawk's foot turned under him with the shock and he pivoted; the brown-toothed outrider stumbled and tripped over his leg, falling headlong against the door. With a yell, he crashed through the wood and fell out into the air.

The outrider's shot went wide as the boxcar shook under him, the bullet carving a score inches from Tyler's feet. He yelped and lost his balance for a second, coming dangerously close to the lip of the roof.

"Whoa!" he called out, his hand catching on a rain guide. Tyler recovered and shifted himself back up. With a grunt of effort, he took a chance and leapt forward to the next carriage. He landed running and kept going. Ahead of him was the coal car, and beyond that, the ominous ebony locomotive.

Yu Lim dropped into a fighting stance as Bear-coat recovered and stabbed at her, the knife shining as it danced towards her. She ignored the rolling of the train; her *sifu* had taught her to fight standing on one leg, so maintaining a footing was child's play. She gave the outrider a sneer of disdain as he stumbled a little and over-extended his reach. Fivehawk reached her in time to see the Chinese girl's arms lash out in a blur. There was a crack like a snapping branch, and Bear-coat cried out; his arm had gained an extra joint where Yu Lim had broken it just above the wrist. With a growl issuing from his throat, the outrider came back at her, swinging his hand like a meaty club. The girl's response was almost balletic;

126

she slipped inside his guard and chopped at his neck, her hand flat like a blade. Yu Lim connected with a nerve bundle and his eyes rolled back into his head. Like a sack of potatoes, he dropped to the wooden floor in an untidy heap.

She flashed Fivehawk a quick smile. "What happened to the other one?"

The Indian indicated the splintered door. "He went to get his gun."

Tyler shook off the creeping cold in his hands and hopped down to the rear of the coal car. It was a good few feet lower than the carriage, and the landing made him wheeze. He came down badly, one foot on the black metal plate of the wagon, the other sinking up to his knee in the coal hopper. He made a quick survey of the coal car and the engine; as with all the other carriages, a single connecting clamp held them together, but unlike any other steam trains Tyler had seen in his life, the Black Train's driver cabin was hardly visible, merged into the shape of the locomotive's streamlined, bullet-shaped fuselage. He would have to negotiate the frosted pile of coals to reach the train's controls — there was no other way ahead.

This close to the engine, the chugging heart of the Black Train was deafening, the unchanging song of the machine filling the air with smoke and soot. Tyler drew his Peacemaker and started forward, doing his best to skip lightly across the shifting mass of black rocks.

A gunshot keened off the metal walls of the wagon, making him twist to one side. He fired back blindly and buried a round in the wood of the trailing carriage. Skale, his teeth bared, appeared like a skull-headed phantom amid the smoke. He leapt at Tyler, his coat fluttering open, and the gunslinger fired again. The bullet struck home, hitting the outrider in the gut. Skale fell face-first into the coal pile, sputtering.

He clutched at his stomach, dark red-green blood spilling out on to the stones. "C-curse you!"

Without warning, Tyler felt the pebbles of coal shift underneath him. Suddenly, the rocks were sinking, disappearing like grain fed through a funnel. Skale screamed; his legs had vanished beneath the moving sea of coal. Tyler grabbed at the wagon's walls and dragged himself up, but he was unable to look away. Horror-struck, he watched the injured outrider disappear under the coal like a man sinking into quicksand. As if in reply to the terrible scene, the Black Train's ear-piercing whistle sounded a single note.

The young gunslinger fought down the churning dread in his chest and vaulted over the lip of the coal car. Laid out before him was the half-open cabin where on any conventional locomotive the engineer would have worked; but Drache's machine was like nothing else on Earth, and Tyler found himself wondering if Fivehawk and Yu Lim might not be right about it being alive somehow. Where there should have been gauges, levers and valves to regulate the locomotive's boiler, there was only a snarl of pipes, clustered around the glowing maw of a vent grille. The machine shot thin spurts of steam at him, hissing like an angry cat. All his thoughts about stopping it died in his mind; he knew with cold certainty that no human being had ever driven this unholy construction of dark iron.

The door to Drache's private carriage splintered under Fivehawk's foot and they entered. Both of them could not help but hesitate as they took in the opulent surroundings, the interior's rich décor of leather, wood and polished metal.

"This is a room fit for an emperor," said Yu Lim.

"Evil often seeks riches," Fivehawk replied. "But gold is no match for a strong heart."

"Indeed." She moved though the room, her eyes scanning every inch of the carriage. "There are hundreds of books. What we seek could be in any one of them." Yu Lim waved a hand at the numerous bookcases around the walls.

The Indian shook his head. "No. Look here." At the opposite end of the carriage was an ornate door of mahogany and brass. "This is Drache's inner sanctum. We'll find his secrets there."

Yu Lim's sword whispered from its scabbard. "Allow me." With a spark of stone on metal, the jade blade cut the hinges from the door and it fell open.

Fivehawk and the girl exchanged glances. "We are in the tiger's lair now."

Tyler dropped back from the roof of the train and in through the shattered door to the passenger carriage. He gave a wry smile when he saw Bear-coat's unconscious form. "Well, well. I guess I must have missed that dance…"

Tyler drew his gun and reloaded his bullets, placing a few unspent rounds in his pocket. Each had a tip of greenish stone. "Not many of these to go around – I better save them for when I need 'em," he said to himself.

He glanced out of the window; the trees and foothills were now long since gone, and in the distance he could see a faint glow of light, near the peak. "Not long now."

Unseen by the gunslinger, a figure hid just outside the carriage, peering through a slit in the half-open door. Ryder held his breath. *Yeah*, he thought, *Not long*.

Drache's study was strewn with papers and plans of all descriptions, but Fivehawk knew instantly when Yu Lim had found what they had been looking for; her gasp was one of shock and surprise.

"What is this?" he asked. In her hands, Yu Lim held a map of the county with the railroad Drache had constructed outlined in heavy lines. To the Indian, the complex snarl of shapes was incomprehensible.

She nodded slowly. "Oh, Jonathan, this is worse than I could have imagined…" She traced the shape with a finger. "Once this track is complete, nothing that lives within its borders will survive."

9: END OF THE LINE

Tyler made his way into Drache's personal carriage and gave a low whistle at the fancy furnishings within. From the next door ahead he heard voices, and the gunslinger cocked his pistol.

He gave an audible sigh of relief when Fivehawk and Yu Lim emerged. "I thought for a second there were more goons on board."

The Indian shook his head. "There were two."

Tyler mimicked Fivehawk's movement. "Uh-uh. There were three. That skinny-looking guy came after me."

"You shot him?" Yu Lim asked, eyeing his gun.

"Yeah, not that it did much but slow him down. These outriders take a lot more lead to put them under than any regular man would."

"He is still alive?"

"Oh no." Tyler looked away, still disturbed by what had happened to Skale. "We were fighting in the coal wagon and it just ... swallowed him up." He shivered, and shook off the memory. "How about you? I saw your handiwork next door..."

"You were correct when you said that Drache would keep plans of his schemes," Yu Lim said, holding up a roll of paper. "We found a map." She unfolded the sketch.

Fivehawk's eyes widened. "The track seems to focus at the end of the line, atop the peak."

Tyler's eyes narrowed. "What in tarnation is that? It looks like a squiggle and a stick-man in a box with a hat on it!"

"It is a pictogram, a character from my language. It is one of the forbidden symbols," said Yu Lim.

"Why would Drache create his iron road in this shape?" Fivehawk traced the edges of the lines. "Look closely, Tyler. Does this shape seem familiar to you?"

The cowboy's mouth dropped open in surprise. "I'll be... When I saw part of the railroad track from the mountain yesterday, it looked like that bit there!" He rocked back on his heels. "That Drache is plumb loco. Someone else might carve their name on a tree trunk, but he writes a Chinese word so big only the birds could read it!"

"You do not understand!" Yu Lim said urgently. "This shape – it is evil!"

He snorted. "How can a giant scribble be evil?"

"My language uses characters like this one to denote the energy of the earth itself. We call it the *qi*, the living essence of nature, of all life." The girl's lips thinned. "In China we believe all things are made up of the elements – earth, wood, water, fire and metal, all in harmony with the *qi*."

"The what? Key?" Tyler repeated.

"The force of life!" Yu Lim snapped. She stabbed her hand at the map. "When this symbol is drawn in metal, it becomes powerful enough to drain the living energy from everything around it. The rails, they will conduct *qi* like they would the heat of a fire, drawing it in from their surroundings." She shook her head. "Can you not see, Drache's railroad was never meant to go anywhere! It will suck out the vitality of this land like marrow from a bone!"

Tyler shook his head. "A magic word," he said flatly. "Girl, you are worse than Fivehawk with this hocus-pocus stuff!"

Yu Lim threw up her hands with a sharp "Ha!" of exasperation.

"Tyler, listen to me," Fivehawk broke in, "whatever you believe is real or not counts for nothing now. You know as well as any of us that Drache's heart is corrupt."

"There's no doubt about that fact," the gunslinger admitted. "Bad is still bad."

"We must stop him. That is the only truth we need to agree on." Fivehawk glanced out of the window. The speed of the locomotive was lessening. "You managed to slow the train?"

"Not exactly. It's kinda hard to put on the brakes when there are none. When you said this thing drives itself, you were right. There's no engineer, no driver, no controls … no nothing. Must be some kinda clockwork."

Yu Lim peered through the window. "Then why are we stopping?"

Fivehawk let his bow drop from his shoulder and into his hands. Outside the window, the glass dome of the terminus hove into view. "Because we have arrived."

The Black Train halted just shy of the glassed-over entrance to the dome and sounded its screeching whistle. Fivehawk, Tyler and Yu Lim did not wait for it to begin moving again, and they jumped into the snow that lay in drifts two feet high alongside the track. Up here on the summit, the air was thinner but still thick with falling flakes and the sting of a harsh wind. Their weapons were at the ready: sword, bow and six-gun.

"A stealthy approach appears to be out of the question," Yu Lim murmured.

Tyler grinned in spite of the fear in his gut. "Ah, we always seem to end up going in through the front door anyhow."

"Then let's end this," Fivehawk said, his voice a low growl. "Drache will pay for his crimes, I swear it."

Yu Lim and Tyler exchanged glances in a moment of shared concern; what would the Indian do if his sister confronted him once more?

As if in answer to the unspoken question, a woman's voice broke through the cold air. "Brother? Are you there?"

"Amber!" Fivehawk started forward in a run.

Tyler stumbled after him, his hand outstretched. "Fivehawk, no! It's a trap!"

The Indian halted in his tracks, his bow pointed at the ground, his face a battleground of conflicting emotions. As Yu Lim and Tyler moved to his side, a trio of shadowy figures emerged from the driving sleet.

Targa pulled back her hood and tossed her flame-red hair, the motion mimicked by Dawne to her left and Fivehawk's sister to her right. Her two bodyguards each held a wicked blade, a knife almost long enough to be a short-sword.

"Ah, everyone is here," Targa said languidly. "Put up your weapons."

Tyler snorted. "Maybe you should take that blind-fold off, lady. Arrows and bullets versus knives? We appear to have the advantage."

"Not quite," Ryder grated. Yu Lim spun round to face him with her sword. Emerging from the train behind them, the outrider aimed a stubby pistol at her. "Four to three. You lose."

"We will never surrender!" Fivehawk took a step forward, his face like thunder. "Never!"

"Oh, really?" Targa asked. She inclined her head toward Eyes-Like-Amber. "Duske, my dear?"

Amber seemed to twitch, and hesitated a moment before answering. "Yes, Governess?"

Targa could barely stop herself from smiling as she spoke. "Take your blade, and cut your own throat."

Amber gave a slow nod and raised her hand, pressing the sharp edge to the soft flesh of her neck.

"No!" Fivehawk shouted. "Stop! Please!"

Targa halted Amber with a wave of her hand; a thin trickle of blood began to gather where the knife had rested on the girl's throat. "Put up your weapons, or I will have the redskin's sister gut herself in front of you."

Fivehawk looked back at Tyler and Yu Lim, with pleading in his eyes. As one, they put their weapons away, Tyler's pistol returning to its holster and the jade sword sliding into Yu Lim's scabbard.

Ryder gave a croaking laugh and jumped down from the Black Train. "Hands up, all of you. I see anyone even thinking about reaching for something and you'll be wearin' a marble hat!"

"That's more sociable," Targa said, watching Fivehawk shoulder his bow and quiver, then raise his hands. "Now then. There's someone who is very much looking forward to meeting you all. We shouldn't keep the Master waiting."

Ryder gave Tyler a rough shove. "Move it, trail rat."

The gunslinger said nothing, studying Fivehawk out of the corner of his eye. The Indian was slump-shouldered, the fire that had been in his gaze only moments ago now suddenly extinguished.

Targa led them out of the snowstorm and into the Terminus dome with her servants at her heels, while Ryder followed behind the three captives. Yu Lim found herself wondering why they had not disarmed them, and the answer gave her a chill. *Perhaps Drache does not fear us*, she wondered. *Perhaps this villain might be more powerful than any of us could have suspected.*

For his part, Tyler could not help but be impressed by the scope of the vast construction of glass and iron Drache had built atop the mountain. He had seen whole villages that would have fitted inside the upturned bowl with room to spare, and he craned his neck to follow the line of the supporting pylons and arches from the ground to the apex of the hemisphere. Cables dangled down here and there, all of them humming with quiet power.

Ryder smacked the back of his head. "Eyes down!" he husked. Tyler grimaced but said nothing, looking instead at the floor. He could see where the lines of the railroad extended into the dome proper and up towards the steel wells buried in the ground. Here and there, a few patches of wind-blown snow had settled in the lee of crates and boxes on the gleaming tiled floor, but, surprisingly, the dome's interior was warm. Tyler wrinkled his nose. The air had a greasy tang to it, and the scent of ozone. The twinkling light of hundreds of gas lamps cast an eerie glow around the atrium, highlighting the patterns of green tiles in among the plain white.

In the very centre of the Terminus, Drache stood on a wide circle of shiny tiles, at the mid-point of an emerald-coloured star. At his feet was an iron frame, supporting a bulbous hidden object covered with a silk cloth. Tyler felt his mouth go dry as he picked out the shapes of a dozen Guardians prowling around the rail baron like a canine honour guard.

Drache smiled broadly, showing a mouth full of teeth. "Ah, my guests. Welcome to you, one and all." His voice was metered and gentle, and for a second Tyler found himself wondering if this well-spoken man could possibly be the same blackheart he had learnt to live in fear of.

Drache stepped a little closer to them and Targa retreated away. "At last we meet." He addressed them, "Jonathan Fivehawk. Gabriel Tyler. I must confess that you certainly don't look like the type of men who could cause me so much trouble."

Tyler spoke before he thought. "Yeah, you're not what I expected, either. I was thinking you would be taller."

Drache raised an eyebrow. "You'll find I'm bigger than I look, Mister Tyler. Much bigger." He glanced at the Indian. "And you, Mister Fivehawk? Do you have a glib comment for me as well?"

Fivehawk stared Drache in the face, his thoughts churning. After his entire journey, after all of the prophecies that Sleeping Fox had told him, he was finally within reach of his enemy. "You will not succeed."

Irritation flickered across Drache's face. "Really? From where I am standing, it appears to me that I most definitely will. And do you know why?" He moved to where Eyes-Like-Amber stood like a blank-faced mannequin. Drache gently traced a hand around her head, his fingers brushing her hair and the obsidian clasp that held it to her neck. "It is because I have rid myself of weakness. The weakness of compassion, of love, of all useless emotion." He placed his hand around Amber's throat. "I merely have to threaten to break this woman's neck, and your weakness will make you my servant. Do you understand me?" He smiled as Fivehawk's eyes flared. "Good, I see that you do."

"It must take much bravery to threaten the life of a docile child," Yu Lim said with venom. "Perhaps as much as it does to enslave the innocent to do your bidding."

Drache seemed to notice the Chinese girl for the first time, and behind his black glasses, his eyes narrowed. "Ah yes. You've proven quite hardy, young lady, surviving the snows and the fumbling attempts of my minions to kill you." He gave a small shrug. "I'm not really sure what you're doing here, but whatever your purpose, you have made a grave mistake allying yourself with these two."

Yu Lim swore a curse in her own tongue. "You think so little of life that you can use men, women and children as tools? My people have waited for hundreds of years for you to show your face once again, and by my Ancestors, your life will be forfeit!"

To her surprise, Drache quivered and shook; he burst into laughter, and his guttural voice echoed around the dome. "Oh, child," he said with a gasp, "your arrogance amuses me. Do you not realize that you don't even matter to the great design? You're just a fly in the ointment, a momentary distraction…" He removed his spectacles and his metallic eyes glittered. "You are beneath my notice."

Tyler's cool cracked. "Ah, you're insane! You wipe out whole towns, kill and maim, and for what? All that power and money you got has made you sick in the head! What do you think building this mad toy railway is going to get you?"

One moment Drache was a good eight feet away; the next he was at Tyler's throat, one hand clamped around it. With no effort, he held the gunslinger up off the floor. "You are as ignorant as you are outspoken, Tyler," Drache's voice hissed through gritted teeth. "This is the penultimate task I must perform! I'll draw up the energy of the Earth herself,

141

and then the seed of all the world's ruin will be born!" As if discarding a spent match, Drache released the cowboy, who fell to the ground in a heap, coughing. The rail baron's mood shifted again and he spoke to the dome as if it were filled with an invisible audience, with a faraway look in his eyes. "These are the last days of man's dominion over the land. My benefactor has slumbered for centuries, and now, at last, his time of awakening is upon us."

"The three stars," Fivehawk blurted out. "When three shine as one."

Drache nodded like a teacher with a promising student. "Indeed. When he came to us, your people imprisoned him, caged him. I will release him."

"You'll end the world!" the Indian shouted. "The Faceless will destroy it!"

"Eventually." Drache favoured him with a smile. "But not before he makes me master of all mankind..."

"I will not let you do this." Fivehawk took a step towards him. "The Great Spirit's prophecy has come full circle ... I will give my life to halt this evil!"

"Oh?" Drache said. "But will you give the life of your sister as well? Or those of the woman and your talkative friend? Your compassion is your weakness, Ulanutani Wanderer! The odds are now stacked in *my* favour!"

"Shall I dispose of them, my Master?" Targa ventured.

Drache walked back to the tiled circle, reaching for the silk cloth. "Just the Chinese. Our benefactor wants the other two alive." He pulled the cover away; there, nestled on an iron frame, was the spherical shape of the Instrument, the arcane device through which the rail baron communicated with his master. "Once the circuit has been completed, put her in the well. She will add her life to empower the device." Drache traced his fingers over the orb, moving them down to a massive slide-switch set into the support. With a flourish, he slammed it forward to its first stop and the dome was lit by a storm of sudden lightning.

Tyler shielded his eyes as he got back to his feet, and watched in awe as the disc beneath Drache's feet trembled and then began to shift. All around them, hidden trapdoors in the tiled floor yawned open and extruded ornate steel columns, which began to extend upward, reaching towards their twins which hung down from the glass ceiling. The white and green dais disconnected from the ground and grew into a tower, carrying Drache, the orb and his phalanx of Guardians into the air. The thick minaret mated with the open skylight at the dome's apex with a heavy thud of iron bolts. Captive sparks of green energy flickered between the webs of cable around the glasshouse, filling the air with static; and for a moment, warrior and outrider alike were held in their tracks by the sight of it.

On the dome roof Drache filled his chest with the cold air and gave a belligerent chuckle. Already the Instrument was thrumming with power, and it split open into segments, each one spitting dozens of brassy cables into waiting hollows on the dome's surface. It was hungry, and the rail baron would give it a feast. Drache gripped the switch and rammed it the rest of the way to its closed position; in answer, huge metal gears began to grind into each other beneath his feet.

The Guardians sniffed the ozone-filled air and howled; the snowstorm began to fade away, the clouds that eternally hid Frost Peak slowly dissipating. Drache licked his lips and gazed into the valley, his eyes of brass filigree tracing the lines of the railroad out across the landscape.

Fivehawk shook off the confusion in his mind and took a chance. He reached out for Amber's arm and tugged on it, whirling her around. He felt something in his heart go cold as he looked into her eyes; they were vacant and empty, like a doll's.

"Sister! Don't you recognize me?" He shot a quick look at Targa; the woman was still distracted by Drache's machines. "Amber, please! Just tell me there is still a part of you that can remember!" Fivehawk felt like his heart would burst with the anguish of it, as his mind filled with a sudden realization. If the Eyes-Like-Amber he knew was truly gone, her soul stolen away by Drache, then

Fivehawk would have to end the life of the empty shell he held in his grip. *I cannot murder my own sister!* he raged to himself. *I must reach her!*

Still hunched over from the effects of Drache's attempt at strangulation, Tyler blinked away the after-image of the lightning from his eyes and turned towards Ryder. The outrider caught the movement and waved his gun at him. "Get up, punk! Let's see your hands!"

"What, these hands?" Tyler brought up his arms from where he was holding them to his body. In his off-hand right grip was the Peacemaker, pulled from his holster as he lay doubled-up on the floor. "Surprise!"

The shot was lost amid the clanging and crashing of moving metal, but the bullet struck Ryder in the chest, pitching him over a crate.

"Brother?" Amber's voice was so quiet at first that Fivehawk thought he had misheard. "It is so dark in here. Am I lost?"

He blinked tears from his eyes. "Yes. Lost. I'm here for you."

Amber's face suddenly snapped up and her eyes were alight with emotion. "Jonathan, run!" she cried. "Targa … she's coming back, back into my mind…"

Behind him, Fivehawk heard the red-haired woman shout something.

"You must go!" Amber cried, her face twisted with mental strain. "She's in my thoughts, she sees through my eyes!" She pushed him away, raising the knife in her hands. "Remember your duty, brother! You cannot save me – you must destroy The Faceless!"

"No!" Fivehawk's shout was a pure animal cry of hurt and rage.

"You cannot save me!" Amber repeated; then a fog descended over her eyes and the blade came racing up at him, a flashing arc of steel.

The Indian twisted away, but too late to get completely clear; the knife drew a needle-thin line of red up his cheek.

"Duske! Dawne!" Targa shouted, and like obedient dogs, the two women ran to her. "Drache wants them alive, he'll have them – but we'll beat them to within an inch of it first!" Her hand wandered to the clasp on the back of her neck; in some way that she could not comprehend, Targa's orders, her force of will, were carried from this device to the identical crystal hasps on her two servants. Drache's arcane science in return granted her sight through their eyes – but as Targa had discovered to her cost, a strong emotion was enough to fog her control of them. She shot a look at Duske; she would have to keep her on a tight leash ... at least until her brother was dead.

*   *   *

The harsh grin of victory on Tyler's face froze like ice when the crate shifted and Ryder hauled himself up from the floor, a ragged wound on his chest oozing green ichor. "Is that the best you can do?" he rasped. "Lead? I eat it for breakfast!" He opened his arms wide. "Come on! Let me have another!"

The gunslinger flicked his revolver to his left hand and spun out an empty cartridge. "You want one? I got a special one just for you." In a single quick movement, Tyler drew one of the few special rounds he'd placed in his pocket and slapped it into place, cocking the gun.

Ryder's face showed fear; the outrider realized what Tyler had done. "Wait!"

"Enjoy your breakfast!" Tyler squeezed the trigger and the sky-rock-tipped bullet hammered into Ryder; in the next second, the outrider exploded in a flash of acrid smoke and ash, his final cry of rage echoing around the dome.

Yu Lim grabbed Fivehawk's elbow and pulled at him. "Come on!"

"I can't leave her!" he said angrily. "There's still time to—"

The Chinese girl tugged him through the forest of steel pillars that had grown up around the dome. "Fivehawk, listen to me! If you try to save her, Drache will win! Why do you think she was here?"

"What do you mean?"

"Did you think it was coincidence? Drache knows now that Amber is your sister, and he will use her to distract you from your mission! He is afraid of you, you and Tyler! He knows that only you two can stop him!"

"The prophecy…" Fivehawk breathed.

She pointed back at the tower. "There is a door at the base. You must prevent Drache from fulfilling his plans." Yu Lim sighed. "That is where your destiny lies."

"But Targa … Amber…"

"I remember my *sifu*'s last lesson … to protect one's friends is the ultimate victory. I will hold them off, and try to save your sister."

Fivehawk felt a new respect for Yu Lim and met her eyes. "Targa will try to kill you. You are only one against three."

She gave him a rueful smile. "Better for one family to weep than a hundred clans. Go now. If this battle is my destiny, I embrace it." And then she kissed him, in a sudden burst of passion. "Follow your path, Fivehawk."

With a banshee cry of fury, Yu Lim drew her sword and attacked.

10: THE DRAGON AWAKENS

Within the dome, iron cogs slick with grease shifted along their axles and turned, pushing into one another as the Terminus moved towards its final state. The time was right, the tracks laid to precise positions, even the metal they were forged from had the perfect balance of elements. Drache had searched for years to find a place like this, where minerals and ley lines conjoined – the fools who lived in the bleak, grey little hamlet below had no comprehension that their homes stood on a natural sink of living power. And now his plans to construct the vast symbol were finally complete, every moment since the day he had tortured a Chinese magician into revealing the shape of the forbidden word was at last paying off. He swelled with pride as the Instrument's insectile song built to a cacophony of clicks, like a million crickets all trapped within the sphere, all its segments aglow. Static electricity danced around the dome, crawling up to the apex to flash into the chill air.

"Feast, foul little seed! Gorge yourself on this

vitality!" The rail baron stroked the surface of the orb and his hand went numb where it touched. All around him, the Guardian wolves were giving the object fearful looks, padding around it in little circles, wary and nervous. They howled in low, plaintive tones.

Inside the dome, the last connection shuddered into place. Two huge iron bars telescoped down from the ceiling on oiled gears, dropping smoothly into the waiting maws of the steel wells set into the floor. They pressed home with a deep thump that made the whole glasshouse twitch with shock. Now nothing could stop the design from fulfilling the purpose it had been created for. The terrible symbol that Drache's slave workers had forged across the landscape came alive as every inch of the iron track resonated with an inhuman hunger for life.

Across the valley, over the foothills and snowy plains, something *changed*. Flocks of birds nesting in trees suddenly started as if a gunshot had cut the air, and they burst into the sky in frightened flight. Animals large and small bolted from cover, out of their dens and setts and away into the cold. Like an unseen gas, the symbol's force radiated outward from the railroad, a colourless slick of anti-life. Snow hissed, flashing into wisps of curling steam, and the hard-frozen earth began to turn black and crumble. Hardy grasses that managed to survive winter's worst cold withered and wilted, curling and cracking as they might have done under a harsh desert sun; strong trees that had grown straight and true for decades began to moulder within as decay ate into their cores, splitting bark and spilling thick sap. And for those unlucky enough to stand a little too close to the rails – the symbol drained them dry as well. A worker who knelt by the humming track fell apart like a bundle of parched sticks, a horse and rider became sunken parodies of life, skin turned instantly into drawn leather.

And still the Instrument fed, draining the life-blood of nature from the land.

In the heart of the Terminus the air was gluey and rich with a tang like burnt oil. Sparks of light lit the dome in actinic flashes, random dazzling blasts that made Yu Lim's eyes hurt to look at them. The Chinese girl danced between the steel pillars that had grown up around the atrium; what only moments ago had been a plain expanse of white tiled floor was now a peculiar forest of thick metal trunks, climbing upward to mesh with each other in a canopy of tinted glass. She hesitated in the shadows. Just a few feet away was the base of the tower that had taken Drache to the roof. Yu Lim looked up, and saw a diffuse emerald glow. Her jaw hardened with purpose. Part of her raged at herself, shouting that she should run to the door at the foot of the tower and climb it to face him. Yu Lim wanted so badly to give in to that voice, to face Drache herself and take the jade sword to him, one single swing to behead that monster and end all this pain. Vengeance burnt inside her chest like a firestorm of hate — how many of her people had he killed? The number was countless, and as she fought to control her emotions she saw poor Tong Biao's face once again, the light in his eyes dying as Targa shot him through his heart.

But she had tried once to defeat this demon and almost died, thrown into a canyon filled with the dead. She had seen the look in Fivehawk's eyes, known then that it was the Indian's destiny to end Drache's life, stop The Faceless before its rebirth. Yu Lim had said herself that her mission was revenge; so it would be. She would confront the Redhair Targa and take her life in reparation for Tong and all the others.

Her knuckles were white around the hilt of her blade and she held it up in front of her, like an offering to her ancestors. The weapon shone in the half-light, the creamy jade of the blade like an arc of lightning frozen in time. In China, such a weapon was called a Lion Head Sword, often used as much for exercise as it was for battle. Yu Lim traced a finger down its length, over the hilt and handle to the crimson silk knotted through a loop on the pommel. The jade sword was an extension of her body and mind, her perfect weapon; and as she studied her reflection in the stone blade, Yu Lim heard her teacher's words echo through her mind, *When good is in danger, only a coward would not defend it.*

Close to the tower, Targa barked orders to the milk-skinned woman Dawne, and to Eyes-Like-Amber. Yu Lim took in a breath and launched herself at them; she would draw them away, and allow Fivehawk and Tyler their moment to run Drache to ground.

Dawne saw Yu Lim first, the Chinese girl emerging from behind the support like a ragged-clothed rocket; and what Dawne saw, Targa's blind eyes saw as well.

"Get her!" she screamed, her face red with anger.

The ghostly woman flicked her arms wide, and a pair of short blades snapped cleanly into her open palms from the holsters inside her sleeves. She twisted about to strike Yu Lim as she closed the distance, but the swordswoman dropped into a somersault that threw her back to her feet close to Amber.

"Duske, cut that slattern apart!" Targa snarled, and Amber responded like a jerky puppet, half-heartedly swinging her knife.

"Amber, you are not her slave!" Yu Lim puffed between breaths. "Your brother loves you — resist her and think only of him!"

For a split-second, a ghost of an emotion crossed Amber's face; then it fled and the Indian girl's expression became wooden and empty. She attacked, and this time all hesitation was gone. Yu Lim parried one strike after another, knife and sword singing in combat. She turned in, under Amber's attack, bringing her weapon to bear – and hesitated. *This will be a killing blow!* she thought. *Fivehawk's sister will die if I finish it!* Yu Lim retreated, her attack unfinished, and Amber came on without missing a beat.

Targa watched with a harsh smile on her face. The Chinese girl was squeamish about attacking Duske – so much the better! She directed her thoughts at the Indian woman with all the force she could muster, the device on her neck humming. "Kill her!"

I cannot fight all three of them at once, Yu Lim thought. *I must even the odds*. As Amber closed in, she spun the jade sword to present the end of the handle. The Indian girl stabbed at her and Yu Lim struck hard and fast, the red strip of cloth arcing out as the pommel struck Amber in the chest. Fivehawk's sister stumbled and fell to the floor, winded.

"I am sorry," Yu Lim breathed.

Targa's rage flooded into Dawne's mind with the force of a hurricane. "Don't fail me! I want this yellow-skinned harpy torn apart!" The pale woman nodded once, and charged, her eyes like those of a blood-hungry shark.

* * *

154

Tyler jumped a foot into the air when Fivehawk tapped him on the shoulder. "Holy Cats!" the gunslinger cried, and he cuffed the Indian lightly. "Don't sneak up on me like that! I nearly had a conniption fit!"

Fivehawk ignored his words and gestured towards the centre of the dome. "Tyler, we must go after Drache *now*."

"But what about Yu Lim? Your sister?"

The Indian looked away. "Yu Lim will distract Targa."

Tyler placed his hand on Fivehawk's shoulder. "That's not what I meant, and you know it. Now, if you want to save her, we'll do it and to hell with Drache's hocus-pocus."

Emotion flared inside Fivehawk, and for a moment he found himself swayed, considering it; but then he choked out a reply. "No. I will put my trust in Yu Lim. You and I have to stop Drache." He blew out a shuddering breath. "It is written, and so it shall be."

The gunslinger opened his mouth to argue, but one glance at the Indian's face stopped him short. "Ah, heck, I've seen that look in your eyes before. That's your *Shut up, Tyler* face." He spun the chamber on his pistol and shook his head, as if in disbelief. "All right then, let's do this thing before we both realize how suicidal it is."

Perhaps it was just the mixed emotions of the

moment, but Fivehawk suddenly smiled. "Didn't you once tell me that you like to go against the odds?"

"I did? Man, that was a dumb thing to say." Tyler cocked the gun. "Let's bag this rattlesnake!"

Fivehawk took up his bow and nodded.

Dawne's attack was like a typhoon of blades, and it was all Yu Lim could do to stand her ground and not retreat. From the corner of her eye she saw Targa draw a wickedly curved knife from the folds of her coat and spin it around her fingers; she knew that the red-haired woman would not chance using her gun inside the dome, perhaps for fear of striking a piece of important machinery or hitting Dawne by mistake. So be it – this would be a battle fought and won by blades.

Targa saw an opening and went for it, holding her knife horizontally across her chest. Her weapon was a devious cutter, a crooked length of bright steel with a diamond-shaped cross-section – a wound from this knife would not close like an ordinary cut, rather it would bleed the victim into submission. She pressed the attack, revealing a set of serrated spikes along the knuckle-duster grip of the blade.

Yu Lim let the two of them close in on her. Targa lunged and Yu Lim feinted to the left, but instead of parrying the fierce strike, she used the jade sword to deflect Dawne. In the same instant, she swept her leg around and caught Targa's heel with the flat of her foot; the force of the spin-kick sent her tumbling to the tiles.

The jade sword clattered against Dawne's blades and Yu Lim pushed in towards her; suddenly, the two fighters were only inches apart.

"Stop this!" Yu Lim said, "You are not her servant! She controls you, makes you fight for her!"

Targa rose from the floor and laughed. "You're wasting your breath, girlie. Dawne's not like the redskin's sister, she willingly became my body-guard!"

"Willingly," Dawne repeated thickly.

"She'd killed seven men before we liberated her from the asylum – now she'll do whatever I ask, and in return I keep her poor, broken mind from wandering."

"Broken." Dawne shoved Yu Lim hard, kicking at her shins, and the Chinese girl fell back. Quickly, she came up to guard herself.

"Finish her!" Targa ordered, and Dawne's face split in a cold smile.

As the two men ducked into the yawning doorway at the base of the tower, both of them could not help but shoot a worried look in Yu Lim's direction. The Chinese girl and her opponents were visible through a flashing net of blades as they fought amid the steel pillars. Fivehawk saw she had been true to her word, and drawn Targa away from the tower. The Indian's heart hammered in his chest when he saw the slumped form of his sister, out cold on the tile floor.

"Don't worry," Tyler reassured him, "with all her fancy footwork, I'm sure Yu Lim could knock Amber out without hurting her."

Fivehawk said nothing and turned away. *I must be strong*, he told himself, *If I am distracted, Drache will kill us all and our fight will have been for nothing.*

Inside the tower, it was as if they were in the barrel of a vast cannon pointed up into the sky. The atmosphere stank of ozone and other alien scents that oozed from the thready mess of cables and wires filling the tower's innards.

"There's footholds here," Tyler called, his voice just loud enough to carry over the echoing vibrations that resonated around them. "We can climb."

Fivehawk tilted his head back and looked up at the emerald glow from the top of the tower; it seemed to be an impossible distance from them. Without speaking, the Indian grabbed at the nearest loop of cable and pulled himself up to the next foothold. Across the way, Tyler did the same, and slowly the two men inched their way up the inside of the tall structure.

Yu Lim saw it clearly now: whatever had been human inside Dawne was long since dead and forgotten. The pale-skinned woman's bloodless face was like the visions of vampires the monks had conjured up for ghost stories in her homeland; but perhaps more terrible was the possibility that the nothingness behind Dawne's eyes was already overtaking Fivehawk's sister as well. Yu Lim remembered her promise to the Indian, and hardened her resolve. *I cannot be defeated today*, she told herself. *I will not!*

Dawne slashed at Yu Lim with both short-swords, one cutting on the upward stroke and the other on the downward. The Chinese girl parried one blade with the jade sword, but the other nicked at her arm, cutting an agonizing gash just below her shoulder. Pain hissed out of her clenched teeth and she struck back hard, knocking Dawne's right arm away. Unlike hers, Dawne's blades were connected to her wrists, so nothing Yu Lim did short of chopping off her hands would disarm her. It also appeared that Targa's bodyguards did not share the outriders' sensibility to the sky rock. *That is why she's holding back, letting them tire me out*, Yu Lim realized.

A few feet away, Amber stirred a little; in moments the stunning blow she had suffered would wear off, and Yu Lim would once again have three enemies. The girl brought the sword close to her chest and gripped it with both hands. Dawne saw the movement as a retreat and pressed her attack, arms opening like the wings of a diving raptor.

Yu Lim blew out her breath in a yell and dropped to the floor, her feet sliding away from each other so she landed with her legs stretched horizontally along the tile, the sword held upward like a pike. Unable to halt her headlong run, Dawne impaled herself on the blade and gave a tiny cry of pain. The pale-skinned woman sank on to the sword all the way to the hilt, the stone blade emerging from her back slick with crimson. For a second, the two fighters hung there in a strange balance; then Dawne's body fell to the floor, the puppet's strings finally cut.

Something dropped away from the dead woman's neck; the gem-like clasp that had held her hair detached and rolled away, trailing a spider-web of brass wires with it.

"You wretch," spat Targa in a low, dangerous tone. "You'll pay for that."

Yu Lim looked up. Before her, Targa was slowly unwrapping her blindfold as Amber shakily stood up. The Chinese girl felt her stomach turn over as Targa met her gaze. Where the red-haired woman should have had eyes, there were two black gems the same colour and form as the hair clasps.

With a keening, scratchy sigh the open segments of the Instrument closed, slotting back into one another with a final, ominous click. Drache reached down to the sphere and tugged it free of the iron frame on which it rested with one meaty hand, then held it to his ear. He sneered as he listened to the rattle of noise inside the object, the metallic beehive buzzing that radiated from it.

"Are you sated now, little seed? Your stomach full of precious essence, loathsome little organ that you are?" Drache whispered. "You are my key. You are the spark that will ignite the fire of The Faceless!"

One of the Guardians at his heel turned and looked away with a growl in its throat. Drache hefted the sphere in his hands and turned to follow the animal's snout.

At the edge of the tower's lip, a curved hatch flipped open with a clatter of iron, and a pair of figures emerged, dark silhouettes framed against the green-lit colours of the dome.

Drache's face creased in anger. "You pathetic, interfering pests!" he bellowed, "Why am I cursed to have you meddle with my every endeavour?"

Tyler and Fivehawk had their weapons at the ready. "Your time is at an end, Robur Drache," the Indian said. "You will not awaken The Faceless today."

Drache's anger was replaced by amusement; he gawked at the two men. "Today?" he laughed. "You are more ignorant that I could imagine! You think that my benefactor is here, in this place?" Drache gestured around. "This desolate scrap of ice and rock in the middle of nowhere?" He roared with laughter, and the Guardians joined in with their howls. "Dolts! This is but the penultimate step on the path to his rebirth. Now the Instrument is prepared, I'll take it to the place where he is buried and he will feed on the life within!"

He took a step back from them, retreating behind the line of snarling wolves. "Time and time again, my benefactor has demanded I bring you two to him alive, and I have obeyed, only to have you interfere with my perfect plans." Drache's eyes flashed. "But soon I will no longer be the servant, and I will not obey!" He snapped his fingers. "Seek!" he shouted, and the Guardians came at them in a wave.

Tyler had loaded his Peacemaker with the sky-rock bullets and now he made every shot count as he fanned the pistol's hammer, the air cracking with the sound. For every round fired a wolf was hit, each one of them bursting like a firecracker in a bag of wet ash. Fivehawk's arrows flew true, the first cutting into a beast that dived for his exposed neck, then a second shot straight at Drache's head.

The rail baron was impossibly fast, his free hand a blur as he snatched the flight out of the air inches before his face. Drache's teeth drew back from his lips in disgust as he eyed the stone arrowhead cut from a sky rock fragment. He broke the arrow in two and threw it aside.

"Your foul pets are dead, Drache," Fivehawk said levelly. "Your outriders gone. You have no more beasts left to defend you."

Drache said nothing, just cast a lazy nod to the railroad track by the dome entrance. Tyler shot Fivehawk a questioning look – then they heard the hiss of steam and the crash of iron against iron.

With a shudder of ebony metal, the Black Train's locomotive flexed along its length like a snake, the movement snapping it free of the coal car and carriages. The twin gas lamps above the spiked cattle-pusher at the front of the engine flared bright red, and along the machine's flanks folds of iron flapped open to reveal hidden systems of pistons and hydraulics.

Like a huge metal flower, the Black Train blossomed, petals of steel extending, rods and armatures growing out of the bullet-shaped fuselage, the many-spoked wheels folding downward and splaying out like claws. The forward half of the locomotive became thinner, and it reared up from the rails, the cattle-pusher spikes shifting and moving. The curved sides of the machine unfolded into thin sheets of beaten black iron that drooped and cut at the cold ground where they touched.

With a sudden rush of motion the engine tilted back to point up into the air; jets of steam rushed around its new form in thin wreaths. The Black Train quivered like an animal shaking off the lethargy of sleep and it filled the air with a monstrous roar. Where the blunt snout of the machine had been before, now there was a mouth of sharp, triangular metal teeth around lips dressed with barbel-like spikes; where a blank cylinder of steel had been, a sinuous articulated body was coiled; and from its back had grown a pair of bat-like wings, as wide and dark as the night.

"Behold, the Iron Dragon!" Drache shouted gleefully.

The red lamp-eyes seemed to study Tyler and Fivehawk for a moment. Then, with a crash of metal and a shower of sparks, the mechanical beast launched itself into the air on flaming, rocket-borne wings.

11: ENGINE OF DESTRUCTION

The Iron Dragon screamed as it cut through the frosty air towards them. The vast black wings beat against the wind and it whirled the snow into a vortex. Fivehawk and Tyler reacted together, throwing themselves to the glass dome as the machine passed overhead. Wrought-iron claws made from the spokes of locomotive wheels slashed through the spaces where they had stood, skipping off the building's frame with a flare of sparks. A sharp gust washed over them in its wake, a draught that brought with it the stench of burning coal and soot.

A spectator to it all, Drache laughed. "You thought you had beaten me? Look at it, gentlemen!" He stabbed his free hand at the flying shadow. "Robur Drache is never beaten!"

Tyler rolled over and came up on his haunches, his pistol cocked and ready. "What kinda unholy contraption is that thing?" he blurted out; but Fivehawk did not hear him. The Indian was mesmerized by the mechanical creature as it turned in the air over their heads, describing a lazy arc like a hawk on a thermal.

Images flooded into his mind, welling up from memory. So many moons ago in the town of Stonetree, he and Tyler had rested for a night after dispatching Drache's raiders, and the old shaman, Sleeping Fox, had visited Fivehawk's dreams. As if it were only yesterday, the Indian saw the crazy cascade of forms once again. *A huge winged beast with flanks of ebony iron, a sad-faced woman with eyes like almonds and a sword in her hand.*

He had seen the Iron Dragon before, both the machine monster and Yu Lim hidden in a fog of dream-memory and only now revealed to him. "A vision," he breathed. "A vision of the future."

Drache grunted. "Fool! You have no future!"

The creature reached the zenith of its flight and spun about. In absolute, terrifying silence it dived at them again, the air rushing away as if it was afraid to block the dragon's path.

Tyler aimed his Peacemaker directly at the diving monster. There was little else he could do — the thing was so huge that he couldn't miss. Even as his jaw trembled in fear, he fired. Even as his brain screamed at him to run and run and run, even as his rational thoughts cried out that such a thing as this could not be possible, Tyler brought his hand down over the hammer of his Colt, holding the trigger back and fanning it like fury.

He discharged all six bullets in half as many seconds.

Like angry fireflies, the rounds ricocheted and deflected off the Iron Dragon's steel hide with hollow clangs and high-pitched cries, never even making the shallowest of scratches. Tyler heard the click of an empty chamber echo in his ears and the machine was on him, crashing into the structure of the dome, puncturing it with peals of broken glass and tortured metal.

"Tyler!" Fivehawk shouted, the shock knocking him into action. He let an arrow fly at the beast, where it bounced away uselessly. Cracking the chill air with its motion, the Iron Dragon's black wings gushed flame and once more it was airborne, leaving a gouge in the dome where it had briefly alighted. Fivehawk did not need to look up to know that the machine would soon turn about and dive after him.

Drache curled his lip in a sneer, but a fresh chuckle died in his throat as the Instrument stirred in his hand. He frowned. The thing was becoming impatient already, and even without the painful business of communing with it, Drache had come to understand something of the device's "moods". He ratcheted a lever hidden in the lee of a stanchion and pulled it to an upright position. With a series of staccato clanking sounds, a set of stairs and a length of guide chain unfolded from one of the dome's supports. Drache cast a quick look back at the Indian and the damage rent by the Iron Dragon. His enemies were finished.

As he stepped lightly down the outside of the glasshouse, Drache held the sphere to his chest like a precious child. By the time he reached the ground, his thoughts were filled with dreams of power and empire no mortal man could ever have conceived.

Fivehawk's heart leapt into his mouth as he peered over the edge of the hole in the roof. He'd half-expected to see Tyler's broken body on the tiled floor far below; instead, there was the gunslinger, clinging to a bent girder, white-faced and wide-eyed.

"Don't just stand there looking at me!" he yelled as soon as he saw the Indian. "Pull me up!"

Fivehawk did just that, more than a little amazed at the cowboy's luck. "What is it that palefaces say about having nine lives like a cat?"

Tyler clenched his hands into fists to stop them trembling. "Oh yeah? Well, I just used up a half-dozen of them!" He glanced up. "Here it comes again! Scatter!"

Both of them dived in different directions as the dragon's vast form swept past, its wingtips kissing the glass dome with a jarring scrape.

"Will you please explain to me how in the Far West a steam train can turn into a lizard with wings?" the gunslinger panted, quickly reloading. "I fired six shots at it, six of your so-called magic bullets, and that didn't even slow it down! We'll need a cannon to blow that thing outta the sky!"

But Fivehawk wasn't listening. "Where is Drache?" he growled.

Tyler looked up – the dais was empty.

Before, Amber had moved like a stiff-jointed old woman, but now she was fast and dangerous, her knife hissing as it cut through the air. Yu Lim saw Targa from the corner of her eye, watchful, waiting for an opportunity to strike at her. The flame-haired woman was directing all of her mental effort into Amber, every last bit of her rage and hate to make the Indian girl a living weapon.

Yu Lim danced back a few steps, swinging the jade sword in a warning arc, but Amber came on, the two blades meeting as she advanced. The Chinese girl frowned; she was purely on the defensive now, parrying each blow as they rained down on her. She watched Amber's dead eyes and saw no expression there. Yu Lim knew that with just a quick twist and reversal she could turn her blade on the girl and pierce her heart … but then Eyes-Like-Amber would be dead and her promise to save the life of Fivehawk's sister would be broken. *I cannot hold her off for ever*, she thought, *and what if she cannot be saved after all?* Yu Lim once again saw the sinister shadows that lived behind Dawne's face, the insane evil. *Could Amber have been tainted too?*

Targa spat an order under her breath and Amber cut inside Yu Lim's guard with a vicious swing. Yu Lim dodged, just barely, and the long knife cut clean through one of the cables that dangled overhead. The sundered wires fizzed, electricity still arcing through them.

"Take her, Duske!" Targa snarled. "Annihilate her!"

Reeling, Yu Lim fought to deflect Amber's never-ending attacks. "Amber! I can save you from this if you just listen to me! Resist her! Resist Targa!"

Her words fell on deaf ears. The Indian girl moved in for a killing blow. Yu Lim felt something crunch under her foot and she lost precious balance, colliding with a pillar. Her heel had crushed the glassy lozenge of Dawne's hair clasp, where it lay on the tile. Her mind raced. *I will not kill an innocent!*

With a savage burst of motion, Yu Lim spun the jade sword around and swung it at Amber's neck.

Targa's breath caught. *The witch is going to behead her!*

But the Chinese girl had lived with the stone blade since the day she had been strong enough to wield it, and she was expert with it. With the skill of a master, Yu Lim halted the blade a fraction of an inch before it bit into Amber's neck; her target was not Amber – it was the clasp that clung to her neck like a malevolent crystalline tick.

The impact gouged a thumb-sized fragment out of the device and it tumbled away. Amber froze in mid-strike and Targa reeled back, as if the force of the blow had been transmitted back to her.

Yu Lim met Amber's bright eyes; suddenly, there was life within them again.

"What have I done?" the Indian girl asked. "I would have killed you!"

"You must break free!" Yu Lim urged. "Remove the clasp!"

Amber shot Targa a glance and shook her head. "To do so would kill me…"

Yu Lim nodded; only Targa's death would be enough to release her victims.

"While I see, so does she," Amber said carefully. "If Targa sees though my eyes, she will kill us both … I cannot allow that."

For a terrible second, Yu Lim thought Amber would plunge her knife into her own chest, but instead the Indian girl spun the blade about, bringing the pommel up, level with her head. "Stop her!" she cried, and then struck herself across the temple in a single, powerful blow. Amber's breath sang out of her lungs and she dropped to the floor in a heap, her bright eyes rolling back into her head as consciousness fled.

Targa shuddered and stepped forward to face Yu Lim. "Deceitful creature! I don't need eyes to see you, to destroy you! I'll find you by sound alone!"

Her hand pulled an object from the pocket of her coat and she threw it at the floor. Yu Lim had time to register an egg-shaped projectile before it hit the tiles and shattered, spilling a cloud of black smoke into the air. Within seconds, the dome filled with a dark, heavy fog. "More fair this way," Targa growled, her gem-like eyes glittering. "Now, girlie, we'll end this!"

"Curse that motherless snake! We turn our backs for a second and he lit out hell for Hades!" Tyler snarled.

"No time for that now!" Fivehawk pointed upward. "His beast is coming back. If we stay up here, it will cut us to ribbons."

The gunslinger gave a sharp nod. The machine had settled on a rocky crag further up the summit, and, as he watched, it turned to study them. The Iron Dragon bellowed and spread its wings once more. "Here it comes!"

In the heat of the moment, an idea struck Fivehawk. "Tyler, quickly! Take this!"

The Indian handed him a broken sheet of metal as big as a tray, part of the dome roof that the dragon had dislodged moments earlier. The gunslinger was nonplussed. "What, a shield? That'll be like catching a .38 slug in a handkerchief!"

Fivehawk shook his head and set another similar fragment down on the dome. "Did you ever have a sledge as a boy?" And with that question, the Indian shoved off and raced away down the curve of the dome, the smooth glass and slick snow creating the perfect slippery surface.

Tyler crossed himself and followed suit, lying flat on his plate as it raced downward. His face was a grinning rictus. "Heck, if I wasn't scared out of my wits, this might even be fun!"

Baffled by the strange antics of its prey, the Iron Dragon skipped off the dome and dropped after them, its black-toothed mouth opening wide.

The men hit the snowy ground seconds apart, not so much dismounting as tumbling into a heap. Fivehawk shook off the snow from his coat and pulled Tyler to his feet. "Come on! We must get into cover!"

They ran as the machine's shadow fell over them; they were on the far side of the dome now, on the flat expanse of rock where Drache's workers had slaved to construct the glasshouse. Here and there were rough wooden sheds and collections of building materials, all covered in inches of snow. They dodged between them, barely keeping their footing when the dragon landed heavily behind them, bellowing.

Tyler drew Fivehawk into the shadow of a small hut and they paused, breath panting out of them in white clouds. "We gotta stop this thing cold," he wheezed.

"You said you knew about these steam trains. How would you stop one of those?"

"I tried that already, remember? Besides, that *thing* ain't no steam train. Heck, I don't know what it is—"

With a crash, the hut exploded into matchwood, clawed apart by one swipe of the dragon's paw. Snow and ice were stirred up into brief whirlwinds as it hit the earth, then launched itself back into the sky. The gunslinger got off two quick shots from his pistol, the bullets sparking where they hit.

"I'm just – huh – wasting my ammo!" Tyler gasped as they broke into a run once more. "If we can't figure out how to get the jump on that monstrosity, we're done for!"

They took cover behind a mess of barrels and coils of heavy rope. Fivehawk blinked and grabbed Tyler's shoulder. "Wait a minute, what did you say?"

"I said, we're done for!" Tyler repeated with feeling.

"No, jump! You said jump!"

Tyler pulled a face. "Did that last swipe knock you in the head? What are you talking about, man?"

Fivehawk jerked a thumb at the machine. "The steel beast – it doesn't fly, it jumps!"

Tyler peeked over the top of the barrel, in time to see the mechanical dragon land hard on a nearby shack, crushing it. In a gout of flame, it took off again in a shallow arc, its whistling cry sounding down the mountain. "So what?"

"Don't you see, the machine cannot fly! It just makes long jumps... It is too—"

"Too heavy!" Tyler broke in. "I get ya. But what good does that get us?"

"We are on top of a mountain, Tyler," the Indian said, and pointed. A slow smile crossed Tyler's face as he followed Fivehawk's gesture to the edge of the mesa-like summit.

With the crashing and shaking around them, it seemed as if the dome might fall apart and crush them at any second, yet Targa and Yu Lim circled each other in a careful silence. For blind Targa, the battleground was a landscape of sounds, while Yu Lim blinked at the black smoke that made her eyes run with tears. She struggled not to cough – any noise would bring Targa's blade straight to her.

Only the faint glow of the jade sword was clear to her, and she held it out, as if it were a charm to ward off evil spirits; everything else was a shifting dark nothingness.

Carefully, Targa took slow and deliberate steps, measuring each footfall against the floor, listening to the tortured metal of the dome as it threatened to collapse. Amid the rush of sounds, she picked out the rhythm of Yu Lim's breathing, the flood of air and in and out of her lungs. Her lips drew back from her teeth in a feral smile. Perfect. Even though Drache had taken her vision in payment for her betrayal of him at Burnt Hills, he had still ensured that she was not totally without senses. Until now, she had contented herself by drawing in perceptions though Duske and Dawne – but now Duske had broken her control and Dawne lay dead, so it was to her own sensorium she returned, and the black gems in her eye-sockets that made her more alert than any cat.

I hear you, Targa told Yu Lim silently, *and those breaths will be your last.*

Fivehawk and Tyler dodged another hammer-blow from the Iron Dragon as the machine split a pile of discarded planks into kindling.

"Distract it!" Fivehawk said, pulling on his bow.

"What?" Tyler gaped, as the machine took an earth-shaking step forward. The gunslinger swore loudly and grabbed a wooden pole. Fearlessly, he swung it at the machine like a club, and it connected with the Iron Dragon's chin.

The mechanism's baleful red lamp-eyes seemed to glare at him for a moment, before its jaws snapped at the pole and bit it in half. Tyler blinked. "Whoops."

It wheezed, bellow-like lungs inside the monster's torso sucking in air, and then blew out a thick stream of flame in an orange jet. Tyler twisted away from the heat, the spray of fire melting a streak of snow beside him. "Of course," Tyler said to himself, almost hysterically, "it's a dragon, so of course it can breathe fire!"

But those moments were all Fivehawk had needed, enough time to douse a sky rock arrowhead in powder from his medicine bundle. As the machine reared back its snake-like head to strike, he loosed the arrow and it flashed through the air. Glass tinkled as the bolt hit squarely in the beast's right eye and it hooted in pain, bringing up a claw to scratch at itself. With a puff of gas, the Iron Dragon tore at the ruined socket, sending the broken lamp to the ground.

Tyler scrambled to Fivehawk's side. "I think you made it angry."

The Chinese girl tensed – was that a faint shimmer of human movement to the left of her? Yu Lim extended her reach on the sword and swung it, only to slice through nothing but empty air. She chewed her lip in frustration. *Your eyes can deceive you*, her teacher had once said, *don't trust them*. She nodded in agreement with the inner voice and closed them, placing herself in Targa's position, listening.

Targa was close, her gentle tread taking her to a position directly behind Yu Lim's back. The girl was totally unaware of her stance, standing oblivious with that cursed stone sword waving back and forth in a vain hope of hitting something. Targa held back a cruel laugh and licked her lips. Her curved blade was cool and hard in her hand, the keen edge poised and ready to pierce Yu Lim's body between the shoulders. *Slowly now*, Targa told herself, *just a little closer*. She would stab the loathsome straw-skinned harpy in the back, and be rid of her.

Yu Lim let the world around her become a cascade of noise that fell into the funnel of her mind. *Stretch out with your feelings!* she told herself. She let the sounds form an image of her surroundings; the creaking pillars before her, the sparking cables to her side, and behind ... behind...

Targa drew back the knife and then plunged it forward, her arm sweeping down.

The jade sword moved in Yu Lim's hands as if it had a life of its own, her grip reversing as she turned it about, flipping the blade backwards and shoving it under her armpit. Her enemy was there, and she struck without pause.

Breath hissed out of Targa's gritted teeth as she impaled herself on the bright stone blade; Yu Lim twisted to face her, hands never leaving the grip, and she buried the jade sword in Targa's chest to the hilt.

"I can't die!" Targa rasped, her flawless skin cracking and shrivelling. "I am Targa, Governess of Winterville, mistress and minion of Robur Drache! You cannot kill me!"

Yu Lim's eyes were as hard as diamond. "For the lives of my brothers and sisters, for Tong Biao and every other human being you have murdered, I am their living revenge!"

"Noooaaahhh!" Targa's final cry of defiance spilled into a ragged scream as she crumbled, her once-perfect body turning old and grey in mere seconds, ageing away into scraps of dead flesh and blackened bones.

"To hell, Targa," Yu Lim said grimly. "I'm sending you to hell!"

The woman's flame-red hair turned to ashen filaments, and like the black smoke around her, Targa's corpse evaporated into the air, leaving only a streak of dark soot on the white tiles and a glistening of greenish ichor on the creamy blade.

Yu Lim sheathed her sword and moved to Amber, who hovered on the edge of consciousness. "Are we free of her?" the Indian girl whispered.

As Yu Lim helped her up, something made of black glass dropped from Amber's neck, shattering as it hit the ground. "Yes. Free."

At the highest point of its upward flight, the Iron Dragon let gravity pull its massive form back down towards the mountainside, its one good eye sweeping the landscape for any sign of the humans. At once, it caught sight of Fivehawk, who stood in the open, waving his arms up and down. The machine tilted its wings and plummeted towards him, raising lengthy razor-sharp claws.

"Here I am!" the Indian yelled. "Catch me if you can!" The dragon let out a cry and angled towards him, and Fivehawk ran with all his might, kicking up spurts of snow in his headlong charge.

The steel beast's paws grabbed at him, cutting a chunk of rock into stone chips as it swooped past, a thin tail of metal cables cracking like a whip as it snapped overhead. Fivehawk felt the heat of the monstrous machine's breath wash around him, but did not dare to look back; then suddenly his feet slipped out from under him and he toppled over. His chase had led him off the rocky ground and on to an ice outcropping. In the next second he was thrown three feet as the steely automaton landed almost on top of him, the impact of the touchdown like a tiny earthquake. It snapped at him, then hesitated; the ground beneath them shivered and trembled.

With a cracking sound like the sky splitting open, the thick cliff of ice broke apart. Formed after decades of snowfall had built up on itself, the frozen ledge extended a good twenty feet over the edge of the mountain – and now it gave way, shattering into lumps as big as houses that dropped straight into the yawning crevasse below. The Iron Dragon was a machine, and the nature of the intelligence that drove it was unclear to Fivehawk; but as it fell away, steel claws snapping at the ice, heavy metal wings struggling to stay afloat in unforgiving air, its screams echoed around the valley like the death-throes of any flesh-and-blood creature.

Fivehawk thought for a moment that he would join the monster in its icy tomb, but then the rope he had secured around his waist was pulled taut and he felt Tyler begin to reel him back from the edge.

Far below him, tons of forged iron and cracked ice buried each other in the mountain's cavernous mass grave; and then, at long last, Frost Peak was silent once again.

12: WINTER SUNRISE

They left the dome behind and never looked back,
taking a connestoga wagon and a frightened horse
tethered nearby to carry them down the mountainside. The ride was largely in silence, an odd kind of
quiet considering that they were the victors this day
– and yet by turns they had also lost, and none of
them wanted to admit it. They told each other their
stories of confrontation and left it at that. Under the
canvas cover of the wagon, Fivehawk ministered to
his sister, wrapping her in blankets and fashioning a
crude poultice out of melted snow and herbs from
his medicine bundle. Tyler sat up front, guiding the
ragged horse as it picked its way through the ice and
rock, and Yu Lim sat beside him, her jacket drawn
up to her chin and the sheathed form of the jade
sword held tight to her.

Tyler had only seen snow in his later years, and in
his introspective moments he marvelled at the way it
seemed to deaden the sounds of the world when it
fell – as if the cold sleet could somehow lay a carpet
of quiet as well a coat of whiteness. The blizzard that

had swept in the night before was gone now, the harsh scratchy winds and needles of ice having dropped away with the clouds, and, as the wagon drew around the rocky escarpment, Tyler saw the whole of the valley laid out before him. The ever-present mists that had obscured it were gone, blown away, leaving Winterville and the surrounding foothills naked.

"Something ain't right down there," he murmured.

Yu Lim yawned like a cat. "What do you see?"

Tyler shrugged. "Take a look."

The Chinese girl squinted past him. Below, in the bowl of stone that made up the valley floor, snow was only now beginning to settle once more on the hills and gullies around Drache's railroad track. It seemed like the bright metal of the iron rails had turned black and scorched the earth around them, burnt it dark like the tracks of charred wood a forest fire would leave in its wake. She could see little detail of the township from here, but the light breeze carried the faint peal of a church bell to her ears, and if she looked very hard, Yu Lim could just about make out the specks of tiny figures moving around the streets.

"The people," she said. "What are they doing?"

"They're leaving," Tyler replied.

They passed the clearing where the they had fought the outriders and the Guardians; the barn and the platform-pulley affair were gone and only a few stubs of broken wood remained, sticking out of the snow like corpse markers. If the blizzard or the shock wave from the rails had knocked down the shack, they did not know, and Tyler rode on without stopping.

When they reached Winterville it was late afternoon, and the sun was already dropping quickly towards the horizon, disappearing behind the mountains. Yu Lim had not been sure what to expect – would the hard-faced locals be angry with them for dispatching Drache's minions, or would they welcome them as liberators and heroes? Whatever she had hoped or feared, she was a little disappointed when they rode into town and were largely ignored.

Fivehawk tapped Tyler on the shoulder. "We should head to the inn and pick up our horses."

The gunslinger nodded. "How's Amber doing?"

The Indian wiped his forehead; he was sweating, despite the cold. "Better, I think. She is strong, and the Great Spirit is watching over her."

Tyler nodded. "Still, wouldn't hurt to get her a night's sleep in a warm bed, right?"

Yu Lim listened to them but said nothing, watching the townspeople as they rushed past them, every one of them intent on their own tasks. She saw wagons and horses being loaded with cloth sacks, packs and everything from rocking chairs to cast-iron bathtubs, children swaddled in winter clothes being led by anxious mothers, men who cradled rifles like they were afraid they might have to use them.

Many of the houses and stores that had been alight with lamps and human habitation were now dark and empty, stripped clean of everything that could be carried, hauled or dragged away. Perhaps it was just a trick of the fading daylight, she wondered, but in some places the wooden slats and planks of the buildings seemed to look different, their colours duller and more worn than she had remembered. The grey little town was like a paper model of its former self, a thin and insubstantial thing that might disintegrate in a hard breeze.

At the inn, Tyler and Fivehawk carried Amber into the bar and set her down on a seat. Despite her fatigue, the Indian girl smiled and Tyler was suddenly struck by her resemblance to her brother. Yu Lim followed them in gingerly, holding the sword tightly.

"Hey!" Tyler cried out. "Old man! How about a little service around here?"

The old bartender entered from the backroom and stopped dead in his tracks. "Mercy. I never thought I'd see you again!" His thin-skinned face wrinkled as he caught sight of Amber, and he stepped back. "N-now I don't want no more trouble in here, do you hear?"

"What's going on in this town?" Fivehawk asked, looking around the empty room. The bottles, glasses, even the mirror on the back wall had all been taken away, leaving the tiny saloon hall as bare as a barn.

"I'm getting out," the bartender piped. "Everyone is. You all had best do the same, you don't want to be here when ... well, when the devil himself comes callin'."

"What are you babbling about, you old coot?" Tyler frowned.

"Heck, boy, you been hiding in a cave all day? Didn't you see it?" The old man stabbed a bony finger in the direction of the mountain. "Saint Elmo's Fire it was, bright as a shooting star, lit up the hills for miles around! Fireworks from the mouth of the underworld!"

Yu Lim and Fivehawk exchanged glances. "The symbol," she whispered.

"It's Judgement Day, that's what it is!" The bartender gave an involuntary shiver. "Trees turning black and birds dropping out of the sky. Some folks said they even seen a giant bat up there! It's retribution, that's what it is. Every man jack of us who lived in Winterville, we seen that heathen dandy Drache and his shady outlaws and we took his coin to be quiet about his foul doings, and look what it got us!"

Fivehawk nodded. "You were unwise to trust him. Now you're paying the price."

"No one is staying around these parts no more. Lookit here. This place is cursed!" The old man reached up to the door and tugged on it; with a crack, a piece of wood came free in his hands. "Wormwood, it is! But this morning, it was fine Canada pine, without a knothole or weevil in it!" He cocked a crooked finger at Tyler. "Mark my words, this town is going be struck off the maps and no man'll ever come this way again!"

"Then I guess you won't mind if we stay a night?"

"Be my guest!" the old man said, grabbing a carpet bag in one hand and slapping a bowler hat on his hairless head with the other. "On the house!" On his way out the door, he ducked past another man coming in.

Yu Lim looked up and her face brightened as she saw the newcomer. "Sing Lung!"

The Chinese man returned her grin and hugged her. "Ah Yu! When we heard about the storm on the mountain, we feared the worst. Are you hurt?"

She shook her head. "No, no. These are my friends – this is Tyler, Fivehawk, and his sister, Eyes-Like-Amber."

Sing Lung's face froze. "But she is the servant of Red-hair..."

Yu Lim shook her head. "No longer. Red-hair is dead; I took her life with the jade sword, freed this woman from her control. Tong Biao and the others can rest in peace, Ah Sing. The deed is done."

Tyler patted the girl on the shoulder. "She's a tough one, all right. Fought like a hellcat up there."

"What about the others?" Yu Lim asked Sing Lung.

"When the rails caught fire we all ran to the camp and hid. Some died as the earth was burnt, but the women and children were all saved. After, when the white men began to leave, we came into the town to escape the cold. They didn't seem to care if we stayed."

"Why not?" Tyler frowned. "They think this place is cursed, if that old goat is anyone to go by."

"What will you do now, Yu Lim?" Fivehawk asked. "Your duty is fulfilled, you have avenged your people."

"Drache is not dead. I feel it in my bones," she husked.

Tyler glanced at Fivehawk. "He may not be. But that's not your fight, Yu Lim. You did more than enough."

"Yes," said the Indian, "I owe you my life and that of my sister. But your people need you now."

Yu Lim looked at Sing Lung and he nodded. "We knew you were going to challenge the evil ones, so we chose to wait for you. I came here as soon as I knew you had returned. You are the strongest and wisest among us, Yu Lim."

"I'm a swordswoman." She scowled. "A fighter, not a monk or a magistrate. I'm too young to lead anyone, if that's what you're asking me."

Fivehawk approached her. "Yu Lim, listen to me. By defeating Targa you freed all your people here – they are no longer slaves to Drache's orders or Targa's vicious whims. They are free. Free to go wherever they want."

"But where can we go?" she asked, and for a moment her eyes flashed like a child's, fearful and anxious. "What if I ... if they are afraid to leave?"

"This is America, the land of opportunity," Tyler began. "Until today, you've only seen the worst of it, thanks to that rattlesnake Drache. You can go home, back to China, or you could stay here and find the best of America. You can make it with your own bare hands, do what you wanted to do in the first place and carve a home for yourselves from the wilderness."

"We will follow you, Yu Lim," Sing Lung said. "We have all agreed."

She nodded. "I must think. I'll have an answer by tomorrow."

The night drew in and silence descended on Winterville. Tyler stood by the window and held back a shudder as he surveyed the empty, vacant street. The last time he had been in a ghost town, it had been the place where he had grown up, the population stolen away by Drache's minions – and now this place had suffered a similar, and permanent, fate, the blame for which could be laid at the rail baron's feet.

Fivehawk entered the room and took a seat by the fire. "Amber is sleeping, as is Yu Lim."

"She's a handsome woman, you know," Tyler said, sitting down. "An exotic beauty and no mistake."

"Which one?"

Tyler just smiled. After a moment he spoke again and the mirth faded away. "Y'know, Fivehawk, even after all we did, hooking up with Yu Lim, smashing up that metal monstrosity of Drache's, I can't help thinking that we lost this round."

The Indian nodded. "Once again he eluded us. Three times now he has been in our grasp and he has slipped away. We cannot afford to lose him again." He paused, staring into the flames. "We have little time, Tyler. By the next moon, the three stars will shine as one, and the prophecy will come to pass. We must stop Drache before that happens."

Tyler's face wrinkled, as if he smelt something bad. "How are we going to track that highbinder down?"

"We will find him," Fivehawk said. "We will follow the Spirit Road."

Tyler rolled his eyes. "Whatever you say. Well then, what about that thing of Drache's, the magic ball whatsis?"

"Yu Lim says that symbol he had the workers build out of railroad tracks leeched life from the earth…"

Tyler nodded. "Yeah, I heard that fairy story too.

But what was he really up to? What was going on with that light show and all?"

Fivehawk sighed. "Paleface, you never change. Anything you see you don't understand is either a 'story of fairies' or a 'mirage'. Here, take this." He held out an object to Tyler, and the cowboy took it.

"What is it?" Tyler studied it – a length of iron railroad track, as long as his forearm. But it was too light, like balsa wood. "Where'd you get it?"

"I broke it off the rails with my bare hands."

"That's impossible. No man could do that. You're making fun of me."

"Yu Lim told us that the symbol drained the living energy from nature, from the rocks and trees, even from the metal itself. Hold it tight, Tyler. See for yourself."

The gunslinger shrugged and gave the bar a squeeze. As if it were made of wet sand, the iron rod broke apart in his hands and crumbled into dust. "Holy Cats. This would have to be buried and rusting for nigh on a hundred years to get that way!"

The Indian favoured him with a hard stare. "Do you believe it now? The legend of The Faceless and Drache's dark dominion?"

Tyler blinked and licked his lips. In his journeys with Fivehawk across the West, the gunslinger had seen things that had flown in the face of all that he believed, impossible things that challenged his view of the world, made him wonder about the nature of

191

what was right and wrong. Gabriel Tyler had always been a thinking man, despite his impulsive nature, always one to listen to the rational, sensible explanation of things. He was, and always had been, a sceptic; at least, he had been before he met Jonathan Fivehawk.

"Do you believe it now, Tyler?" Fivehawk repeated.

The moment drew out into a long silence. Then the gunslinger gave a single nod. "I guess I do."

At dawn, Fivehawk nudged open the door to his sister's room. Eyes-Like-Amber stirred gently and turned over, her brown eyes opening. He could not help but smile at her; just seeing the light and animation back in her face raised his spirits.

"Brother, come sit with me a moment." Her face reflected his happiness.

"Of course." He rested on the end of the bed.

Amber cocked her head with a grin and made a play of studying him. "I see your smile and I fear that you have not used it for a long while."

"I did not have you to tease me, dear sister."

"Ah!" She nodded, looked away. "Father will be angered when he hears that you thought of me before your duty to the Great Spirit."

"He will," Fivehawk said. "But then he will realize that I could do nothing less. When Tyler's uncle was a prisoner of Drache, I saw in his face the mirror of my own fears, that the blood of my blood would die before I could save her, save you." He took a breath. "Even in his harshest rages, not even the Great Spirit would have wished that upon any man."

Amber hugged him impulsively. "When Targa controlled me, she shut all that I was in a tiny dark place, battered me away, boxed me up. Whenever I found myself there, I took comfort in one thing – the knowledge that my brother would come and release me from this pain."

Fivehawk blinked away a tear. "I could do nothing less," he repeated.

The siblings held each other for a while, the simple human contact enough communication for them both. Then Amber spoke again.

"What will we do now, my brother?"

"The Umatilla tribe have an encampment a day's ride from here, We will take you there, and then Tyler and I will set out for Drache." He stood up. "For the last time."

"This Tyler… He seems much like you."

"He is nothing like me!" Fivehawk retorted hotly. "You mock me!"

"Perhaps I do!" She smiled and nodded at the window, where the first orange rays of dawn were emerging. "Look, Jonathan, see how the sun rises. You should make your farewells before it climbs too high and the day is lost."

"What do you mean?"

Eyes-Like-Amber grinned widely. "You do not change, brother. You have the heart of a bear, but all too often, the brain of a fish as well!"

Tyler busied himself with making breakfast. It seemed like it had been weeks since he'd had a decent meal, and with some inventive scrounging, the cowboy had found plenty of fixings in the abandoned township. He took a sniff of the coffee he had brewed, taken from a tin left in the general store.

"They sure ain't going to come back for it..." he told himself.

"Come back for what?" Yu Lim asked, approaching. "What are you making?"

Tyler grinned. "Bacon, eggs, a little bread and some beans. Would you like some?" He waved the pan under her nose, and the girl's face soured.

"No, thank you."

The gunslinger gave her an arch look. "So, what do Chinese folks eat, then?"

"Fish, rice, pork ... but nothing so greasy as that!"

He shrugged. "Well, have some coffee instead. This is good stuff, strong enough to float a Colt!" Tyler handed her a brimming mug. "So, are you going to go back to China, or stick around for a while? I was thinking maybe you could teach me some of that fighting stuff you do. What do you call it?"

"*Kung fu.*"

"I beg your pardon?"

She sipped the drink. "I'm not sure what to do, Tyler. Last night I thought about running away … but I couldn't."

"Your people need you," said Fivehawk as he entered.

Tyler looked away. "Uh, well, I made some food here, so why don't you two eat and I'll just, uh, eat mine somewhere else, right?" The gunslinger gave the girl's shoulder a friendly squeeze. "I know you'll do the right thing, Yu Lim. Maybe we'll see each other again after this is all over, hey? Good luck, miss." He doffed his hat.

She smiled back at him. "To you too, Gabriel Tyler."

When they were alone, the silence between them was heavy; with effort, Fivehawk broke it, taking Yu Lim's hand.

"You and I," he said hesitantly. "Our paths met in this place, but now they are about to part once more."

She nodded. "I have chosen to take Sing Lung and the others to safety. You must finish what you started with Drache and the demon." She delicately reached inside her jacket and undid a lanyard around her neck. "I want you to have this." Yu Lim handed Fivehawk a small disc of jade as big as a silver dollar, with a hole in the middle. "This will bring you luck, Jonathan Fivehawk." *Luck*, she told herself, *and something more…*

Yu Lim looked up into the Indian's eyes and kissed him gently on the lips. "Remember me," she said, her voice catching. She took up the jade sword and left him there, staring after her as she walked away into the rising sun.

"Fivehawk." Tyler's words started him from his reverie. The gunslinger gave him a rueful smile. "Don't worry, my friend. When this is all over, we'll come back this way, count on it."

"What do you mean?" the Indian asked, flushing.

"Hey, I know you like her."

"And how can you tell that?"

"Because you let a plate of food go cold so you could talk to her rather than gulp it down like you always do!"

Fivehawk frowned, then asked. "Is there anything else left to eat?"

Tyler laughed and slapped him on the back.

If this place had a name, the last man who had known it was dead, most likely buried somewhere within sight of the horizon; and that scope took in a huge tract of land, a vast, flat wilderness broken only by crooked trees and discarded snarls of fencing. To one who stood here, in this nameless place, it might seem as if they were in a world that knew no mountains, no hills or valleys, no land except endless, endless even ground racing away to the vanishing point. It was marked on no map, given no identity, and yet this place had seen more blood shed on it than any acre of the Earth's soil.

In this wind-blasted flatland lay the very end of Robur Drache's master-plan, the point to which every moment in his dark life had built. A spent horse lay steaming and panting, lying close to death where he had rode it to within an inch of its life. It was the last in a line of animals that he had used up, starting with the ropy old nag he'd stolen at the base of Frost Peak, the horse that had panicked and whined as his bat-winged glider had settled soundlessly to the snowy earth. It mattered little to him that his constructions had been destroyed, the glass dome of the Terminus cracked like an egg, his precious Black Train smashed beyond repair; here was his ultimate goal, and he was within a heartbeat of seizing it. His escape, Drache reasoned, was just another example of his boundless superiority, his intellect and planning allowing him to avoid his enemies and to come here, to the place. The nameless place.

Drache took a last, long look around at the waist-high sea of sharp, spiky prairie grass and beamed. This would be the last moment for the world to be free. From the next, it would all belong to him.

With a flourish, Drache tore open the burlap sack he held and removed its sole contents – the spherical shape of the Instrument. The object chittered and growled, spilling sparks of green light from its surface; it *knew* how close they were to the end. Shouting with the exertion, Drache hefted the Instrument like a shot-putter and threw it into the air.

The sphere hurtled upward, describing a steep arc before abruptly halting in mid-air. With a noise like the birth of a million locusts, the Instrument cracked open and injected hundreds of brass cables into the dull earth. In reply, the flat landscape rippled, as if it were a blanket cast over some huge beast turning in its sleep.

Drache raised his hands over his head and began to weep with joy, tears streaming around the golden brass orbs of his eyes.

"It begins!" he shouted, and the wind wailed with him, snatching his cry away to all corners of the compass.

SUNDOWNERS

Watch out for
the next book in the series

SHOWDOWN

Cooper tipped back his hat with a finger and swatted at another locust as it droned past his nose. "What in tarnation?" he grated, glancing at Abner. "Where are these things coming from?" Todd could see a half-dozen of the bugs performing lazy circles around the stagecoach.

But the old man's attention was fixed further down the road. Cooper followed Abner's look and gave an involuntary start. Some hundred yards ahead of them stood the figure of a man in the middle of the trail, a crumpled hat on his head and his body hidden under the shape of a ragged duster coat. Cooper gestured to Abner to halt the wagon and the old man obeyed. All thoughts of boredom vanished in a moment from Cooper's mind; he was all business now, a soldier.

The sergeant's gaze flicked left to right – there was nothing but a spread of light scrubland to either side of the road, just some gnarled trees and barely any cover for a troop of bandits to hide behind in waiting for them. He carefully dismounted and started a slow walk towards the man on the road. Cooper could see no sign of a horse or any other means of transport – how had this person got all the way out here? The soldier's hand dropped to within inches of the pistol in his belt – perhaps this fellow was some unfortunate soul who had got lost in the plains . . . or perhaps he was a footpad and killer out to gun them all down. Cooper's nose wrinkled as he came closer. Whoever this person was, he smelt *bad*; not just the stink of a man's stale sweat, or even the foul odour of an outhouse, but a gut-twisting, sickly stench like rotting meat.

"Howdy," Cooper began evenly. "You lost, mister?"

The man's head was staring at the ground, and at Cooper's words, he tilted it back to look him square in the face. The young soldier's mouth dropped open as their gazes met. On the man's head was a tattered cavalry officer's hat, ripped and stained with patches of dark brown; but his face was what stopped Cooper dead. The man's jaw hung at an odd angle, as if the bone had been knocked out of joint, exposing broken, yellow teeth; and where his right eye should have been, there was a gaping, empty socket.

Out of nowhere, the wind returned, kicking up twirls of dust into tiny tornadoes. The man's duster flapped open to reveal more torn shreds of clothing, clinging to a pale, corpse-coloured body. Cooper took an involuntary step back, almost tripping over his own feet. The slaughterhouse stink filled his nose, triggering a memory. The last time Todd had smelt that, he had been fighting the Oglala at Slim Buttes, surrounded by dead and injured men.

Abner stood up on the stage's roof and cocked his rifle with a snap. Beneath him, the coach's doors opened to allow Huxtable, Wyner and the Quaker to exit. The Quaker's voice died in his throat as he took in the scene, and he clutched the Bible in his hand to his chest.

From out of nowhere, more men had appeared. Abner squinted at them, his brow crinkling with confusion. All the figures were mud-splattered and dishevelled, but he could still recognize uniforms and clothing even at this distance. There were Union soldiers side by side with a couple of grey-coated Confederates in livery from the Civil War. A rag-clothed Pawnee scout next to a Sioux rifleman with a crooked neck, the two sworn tribal enemies together without a sign of tension between them.

"Who are these people? What is that awful smell?" Huxtable asked.

Cooper found his voice once more, stammering. "N-now, what's all this about?" he quavered, his hand on his pistol's butt. "Suh-speak up!"

The one-eyed man's hand flicked down towards his tarnished gun-belt by way of an answer, and Cooper followed suit. The young soldier was a fast draw, and his Smith & Wesson cleared its holster in a flash. Cooper squeezed the trigger and a bullet hit One-Eye in the chest. The lead shot snapped through his bony ribcage and out through his back in a puff of dust without any other effect; then One-Eye's jaw moved in the approximation of a grin, and he fired his own gun. It was a broken-looking old Army Colt, a long-nosed wheelgun covered in rust and caked dirt, but the blast from the weapon pierced Cooper's heart with deadly accuracy. Abner choked out a gasp as the young lad dropped to the road in a heap, his life extinguished in an instant.

In the next second, the old driver was letting off shot after shot at the menacing figures, years of practice making every round ring true, never missing a target. But they still came, moving like cripples and half-broken puppets on distorted and crooked legs, carrying the reek of decay along with them.

Huxtable, his prim and proper concerns forgotten, grabbed Wyner by the arm and shook him, wide-eyed with fear. "My god, man! Those bullets are passing right through them! What are they?"

"Death!" squealed the Quaker. "Death, reborn from the grave, it is!" He fumbled with his Bible, flipping wildly through the pages, "Judgement day is upon us, and your lawless hedonism has brought it about!"

Wyner reacted with a sharp jab, punching Huxtable in the gut. As the portly man doubled over, Joe turned him about and thrust him at the approaching figures. "Here ya go!" he shouted. "This'll keep you busy!" Barging the Quaker to one side, Wyner grabbed at Cooper's riderless horse and vaulted smartly into its saddle.

"What are you doing?" Abner shouted at him. The attackers were almost upon the stagecoach now, and Huxtable's wife was shrieking.

"You can't leave us!" the Quaker bellowed.

Joe Wyner turned the horse off the road and hit it hard with the reins. "No? Watch me." The animal bolted into the flatlands at a gallop, blowing his hat from his head with the speed of its passage.

After a few miles, the wind thinned out the sounds of gunshots and the screaming.